Sherlock Holmes and the Royal Flush

Also by Barrie Roberts

Sherlock Holmes and the Railway Maniac (1994)
Sherlock Holmes and the Devil's Grail (1995)
Sherlock Holmes and the Man from Hell (1997)
The Victory Snapshot (1997)

SHERLOCK HOLMES AND THE ROYAL FLUSH

A narrative believed to be from the pen of
John H Watson, MD

Annotated and edited for publication by
Barrie Roberts

Constable · London

First published in Great Britain 1998
by Constable & Company Ltd
3 the Lanchesters, 162 Fulham Palace Road
London W6 9ER
Copyright © 1998 Barrie Roberts
The characters of Sherlock Holmes and Dr Watson and all
other characters created by Sir Arthur Conan Doyle ©
Andrea Plunket, 1996, reproduced by kind permission of
Jonathan Clowes Limited, on behalf of Mrs Andrea Plunket.
The right of Barrie Roberts to be identified as the author of
this work has been asserted by him in accordance with the
Copyright, Designs and Patents Act 1988
ISBN 0 094 79240 2
Set in Palatino by Pure Tech India Ltd, Pondicherry
http://www.puretech.com
Printed and bound in Great Britain by MPG Books Ltd.,
Bodmin, Cornwall
A CIP catalogue record for this book is available from the
British Library

CONTENTS

INTRODUCTION

The accompanying narrative is derived from one of a number of manuscripts that have descended to me from my maternal grandfather, who was both a Captain in the Royal Army Medical Corps and a contemporary of Dr Watson in that service.

The manuscripts seem to represent an attempt by Watson in his later years to complete his accounts of all Sherlock Holmes' cases. In addition to the present narrative I have previously edited for publication *Sherlock Holmes and the Railway Maniac* (Constable, 1994), *Sherlock Holmes and the Devil's Grail* (Constable, 1995) and *Sherlock Holmes and the Man from Hell* (Constable, 1997).

It appears impossible to establish with absolute certainty that these manuscripts are the work of Dr Watson, but in an effort to test their authenticity I have researched various aspects of the narratives. Notes on my findings and opinions will be found at the end of the narrative and readers must decide for themselves whether this is truly a hitherto unknown exploit of Sherlock Holmes recorded by John H. Watson.

Barrie Roberts
June 1998

1

A THEATRICAL INCIDENT

In attempting to complete my records of the cases of my friend Mr Sherlock Holmes I am often at a loss to know which case I should describe next. Admittedly, I commenced with 'A Study in Scarlet', an account of the first enquiry in which Holmes chose to involve me, but later I was able to give to the public details of some cases that had occurred before Holmes and I ever met, and I have never followed a strictly chronological pattern. Despite Holmes' criticisms of my published accounts and his accusations that I have sensationalised and trivialised his deductions, it has always been my intention to leave a record of his extraordinary methods and skills. At the same time I recognise that the lay reader does not require a dry treatise on deductive inference and seeks a certain amount of drama in his reading, which I have attempted to supply.

I have in my journals notes of far more than the fifty or so cases which I have written up for publication and, being now in my seventh decade, I must bear in mind that it may not be possible for me to complete the task of reporting all of my friend's cases. My documentary records are so extensive as to make it impossible to review them in detail and to place the cases in some order of priority. I must trust to memory to recall to my attention cases which seemed to be particularly significant, curious or dramatic, and sometimes memory itself is prompted in the strangest ways.

I was recently in Aberdeen, a city which I had not visited since I accompanied Holmes there on his last case.* I had gone on this occasion at the invitation of my old colleague Stamford, to deliver a lecture at the Medical School of the University on the treatment of some of the appalling cases which are returned to our hospitals from the Western Front.

* See *Sherlock Holmes and the Railway Maniac*, Constable, 1994.

I do not think it would be immodest to say that my lecture was well received by the students. In the evening Stamford and I dined in the college's refectory where, after the meal, the students behaved much as I recall my contemporaries doing forty years ago in London. A group of them performed a short play, which entirely bewildered me until Stamford explained that it was a reconstruction of the fate of one Downie, once a porter at a college in the city.

It seems that this man made a practice of spying on the students and reporting their least misdemeanour to the college authorities. At length the students decided to punish Downie. Seizing the porter one night, they dragged him to a college cellar and brought him before a solemnly robed and hooded committee, where he was informed that he was to be tried for his practices. A 'trial' of his offences then took place, at the end of which the unhappy wretch was informed that the sentence was a capital one and that he was to be decapitated with a razor. As his captors held him kneeling before his judges, the edge of a playing card was drawn across the terrified porter's exposed neck. So great was his fear that he fell dead from shock at the touch of the card's thin edge.

After this gruesome little melodrama the students took to singing, many of their choruses being ones which I recalled from my own youth and in which Stamford and I could join with enthusiasm. There were, however, others which were unknown to me, including one which followed a fulsome speech of thanks to me for my lecture and for publicising Holmes' exploits, ending with a toast to 'Dr Watson and his friend the Great Detective – Sherlock Holmes'. The entire refectory then joined in a curious comic ballad dedicated to my friend. I confess that I felt touched that he was so enthusiastically remembered by young men who must have been little more than children when he retired from practice. It made a pleasing end to my day in Aberdeen.

On my journey back to London the next day I was turning over events in Aberdeen when there returned to my mind a snatch of the students' song which alluded to Holmes playing at cards (an occupation which, incidentally, he regarded as a complete waste of time). By one of those strange spirals of association which the mind forms, the lines brought to mind the card-player's expression 'a royal flush' and a case of my friend's in which that phrase was to acquire the most sinister connotations.

The case of the 'royal flush' occurred thirty years ago, in the year of the old Queen's first Jubilee, 1887, a time when I had not yet met the lady who was to become my wife and when I was still in my first period of residence with Holmes at Baker Street.

Late in April of that year Holmes had dealt with the case which I have recorded as 'The Reigate Squires' and, in its immediate aftermath, had no particular investigation on his hands. He had, I admit, said that our interlude in the country had left him refreshed and invigorated, but he was at that time a self-poisoner with cocaine, a practice of which I strongly disapproved though a number of Continental medical men were still prepared to assert that the drug was entirely harmless. I was always concerned when he had no enquiry to pursue, for it was on such occasions that the cocaine syringe served as a substitute for intellectual stimulus.

I was, therefore, well pleased when Holmes himself suggested that we should take a Turkish bath. Invigorated by the steam room we decided afterwards to enjoy the smiling spring morning by walking back to our lodgings. As we came up Baker Street we became aware of a small man walking ahead of us with a folded newspaper beneath his arm.

'Hullo!' exclaimed Holmes. 'I do believe that Lestrade is on his way to call upon us.'

At this period Inspector Lestrade had not developed his later practice of dropping in upon us of an evening. That only began when he had finally become convinced that my friend's methods of analysis were of value, after which belated discovery he would frequently recite to Holmes the details of enquiries in which he was engaged and receive in return my friend's pointers as to the directions and measures which he should take. Lestrade would relay to Holmes the latest news and gossip from Scotland Yard, which Holmes accumulated as enthusiastically as he sought similar information about the criminal classes of Whitechapel.

I was a little annoyed on my friend's behalf, for too often I had seen Lestrade call upon Holmes as a kind of last resort and, having been given sound advice, treat the successful outcome to which it led as some form of luck. Nevertheless, Holmes greeted the little detective affably when we met at our doorstep and took him up to our sitting-room.

'Take the basket chair, Lestrade,' he invited, and offered the Inspector a cheroot from the coal-scuttle. 'Now, what insoluble case brings you here at this hour of the day?'

'I have no cases, as such, at present, Mr Holmes,' said Lestrade. 'You may know that Dolly Williamson at the Yard has a bee in his bonnet about Fenians or Anarchists seeking to commit some kind of outrage during the celebrations for Her Majesty's Jubilee. So a number of us have been detailed to work under Mr Littlechild. While his officers are going about trying to sniff out such a plot, we are assigned to keep watch upon various foreign notables in London and protect them from any kind of attack. It seems to me that thieving will run riot all over London while we're hanging about looking to prevent murders that aren't going to happen anyway,' he finished gloomily.

Holmes was filling his pipe from the Persian slipper in which he always kept his tobacco. 'It certainly seems', he said, 'a pointless exercise unless Littlechild has some very good information.'

'There's the rub, Mr Holmes,' said Lestrade. 'So far as I can tell, Littlechild has only a rumour passed on by an informer. You know what informers are, Mr Holmes. They'll tell you anything for a few shillings.'

'Undoubtedly,' agreed Holmes, as though he had never paid for information. 'If you have no cases at present, how can I assist you?'

'Well,' began Lestrade, 'though I have never fully agreed with your approach to detection, Mr Holmes, I have to own that you do have a remarkable fund of out-of-the-way knowledge, such as a police detective hasn't the time to accumulate. After reading this morning's paper and being in this vicinity, it occurred to me that you might be able to explain a point or two in connection with something that occurred last night.'

'And what was that?' asked Holmes.

'Well, Mr Holmes, in pursuit of my new duties I was sent to the theatre last night, to provide protection for the American Minister and a party of American visitors to London. I can't say as I found the play very enjoyable, nor was there any sign of Anarchists or Fenians that I could detect, but as Mr Phelps' party was leaving the theatre there was an incident in the lobby that caused me and my colleagues a certain amount of concern.'

He drew on his cheroot. 'As I say, the Minister and his party were leaving when an old man sprang up from nowhere as it seemed and began to shout at one of Mr Phelps' guests and started to try and attack him.'

'Who was the guest?' enquired my friend.

Lestrade took out the newspaper which he had slipped into his coat pocket, unfolded it and glanced down a page. 'He was a Mr Sempford Candover, Mr Holmes. I believe he is a big financier in America. He has been in London on business and is staying for the Jubilee.'

'And what happened when the old man tried to attack him?'

'Luckily the old fellow started shouting out before he got to Mr Candover, so we were alerted to the danger and he never really got his hands on him.'

'What was the old man like?' asked Holmes.

'He was thin, with a sort of yellowish complexion, as if he might have been in a hot climate, and he had a great thick white beard and long white hair. He had thick white eyebrows and the most piercing black eyes I have ever seen, Mr Holmes.'

'And how was he dressed?'

'He was quite respectably dressed in a bit of a strange way.'

'A strange way?' queried Holmes. 'What was strange about his dress?'

'Well, Mr Holmes, he had a very highly coloured waistcoat, such as you don't usually see on men of his age, and a dark cape, very long and wide, not the usual gentleman's evening cloak. When I first saw him he was wearing a wide-brimmed black hat, rather foreign-looking I thought, as it might be Italian perhaps, but that came off in the struggle. He had a stick in his hand, but again it wasn't an ordinary sort of evening cane, it was a long stick with a big silver head to it. I was worried that he

11

might do someone some harm with it, but he didn't get the chance to use it.'

'And you say his attack was entirely directed at Mr Candover? Not at the Minister or anyone else in the party?'

'Oh no, Mr Holmes. There was five gentlemen with Mr Phelps, including Mr Candover, and then there was the ladies of the party, but this man was all out after Mr Candover.'

'You say he was shouting. What was he saying?'

'Ah, now there is my little problem,' said the Inspector. 'By the time I got close to him, people were pulling him away from Mr Candover and he was making what I can only describe as unintelligible sounds. Now I was for taking him into custody and at the least getting him bound over to keep the peace, but Mr Candover made light of the affair and said that he didn't want some deluded old man being locked up. He said that these things happened in America as well and the people involved were usually harmless lunatics. Mr Phelps, the Minister, said that I was to do whatever Mr Candover wanted, so I had to let the old fellow go, though I did give him a pretty strong warning about the way he conducted himself in public.'

'Did Candover know the old man?'

'No, Mr Holmes. I asked him and he said he'd never set eyes on him before.'

'So, a prominent American visitor to these shores was the target of an attack by some kind of elderly lunatic, but no harm occurred and the old man has been let go. I confess that I do not really see a problem,' said Holmes.

'It may be that there isn't one,' said Lestrade, 'but I can't help feeling that if Mr Littlechild is right, then that old man might not be so harmless as Mr Candover believed. He might, let us say, have been set on to draw me and my colleagues out, so that someone would learn the extent of the police protection to foreign notables.'

Holmes sucked at his pipe and nodded. 'True,' he said. 'But what has this morning's newspaper got to do with it?'

'You asked what he was shouting, Mr Holmes, which I did not hear, but according to this report the writer did catch some of his remarks. Now they include words and names that seem very strange to me, so that I wonder if the reporter has not imagined them, but nevertheless, I thought that if you could assist me in seeing what they might mean, I could set my mind at rest as to whether he was a harmless lunatic or not.'

'Very wise,' said Holmes and held out his hand for the news-paper.

My friend took it and scanned the page. 'One of the radical sheets, I see. No wonder that I had not seen it this morning. There is a headline – "A Theatrical Occurrence" – followed by an account of the play. I see that he agrees with your view, Lestrade, that it was not greatly entertaining. Then he goes on to the incident in the lobby.'

He read aloud: '"Among the many prominent persons in the audience were Mr Edward J. Phelps, the American Minister to London, and a party of his fellow countrymen who are here to see us celebrate our Queen's Jubilee. One is always amused at the attention which our transatlantic cousins bestow on a form of government which they rejected violently more than a century ago.

'"Mr Phelps' party had come down to the lobby of the theatre when a gentleman of the party was attacked by a strangely dressed old man who had something of the aspect of an Old Testament prophet. Hurling himself at Mr Candover, the Minis-ter's guest, the old man uttered cries of 'Ashtaroth! What did you do to Ashtaroth?' and 'Herod! Poor innocent Herod! Their blood is upon you and that of Mary who died dreadfully for nothing! Holy innocents! Holy innocents! You drove John out of Egypt and when he knew of her fate he wept and vowed vengeance. Oh, poor Sohrab, poor Sohrab!'

'"Bystanders and plainclothes police officers intervened to prevent any harm to Mr Candover, who was not disposed to treat the matter very seriously. He refused to lay any charge against his attacker and told our representative that 'Being well known through the press makes a man a natural target for the lunatics of this world. They are invariably harmless and always either poor creatures who have taken religion or politics too seriously.' In answer to our reporter's question he smiled and replied, 'Sir, both religion and politics are serious matters, I have no doubt, but my business is money and that is a really serious matter.'"'

'Who was Ashtaroth, Watson?' asked Holmes when he had read the extract.

I cast my mind back to schooldays. 'Is it not', I asked, 'an alternative name for the goddess Astarte?'

'Of course,' said Holmes. 'The Semitic equivalent of Egypt's Isis, a goddess of fertility, or of Diana. Not usually found in the company of such New Testament characters as John and Herod and Mary, let alone the Persian Sohrab. What, I wonder, was Mary's dreadful death? I recall no account of her end.'

'I seem to recall a story that the Mother of Our Lord ended her days in France,' I mused, 'but I don't remember that there was anything very terrible about her death.'

'Really, Watson,' exclaimed Holmes, ungratefully, 'you do fill your mind with the most extraordinarily useless information!'

Lestrade had watched this exchange in some bewilderment. 'What I need to know, Mr Holmes,' he said, 'is what you make of those remarks. Is there any indication that the man was other than a harmless lunatic?'

Holmes looked over the newspaper report again. 'It seems to be a case of religious mania, some delusion that has led the man to identify Candover as the enemy of his distorted faith, but I would not ignore him entirely. He could, as you suggested, be more than he seems. Do you have his address?'

'Yes, Mr Holmes. He lives in lodgings, close to the British Museum.'

'Ah,' said Holmes, 'the haunt of many a lonely scholar with a strange obsession.'

'Should I have him watched, Mr Holmes? I could get Mr Littlechild to put a couple of his men after him. They're used to sneaking about disguised as layabouts,' he said, with a slight note of scorn.

Holmes shook his head. 'No, no,' he said. 'Keep him in mind and watch for any further appearance he may make. If he requires watching I shall undertake that duty.'

'The Secret Branch could do it,' repeated Lestrade.

'No doubt,' said Holmes, 'but they would not do it as secretly as I would, and it would be a pity to arouse his suspicions if he is indeed engaged in some plot. Just keep an eye out for him, Lestrade, and leave the rest to me.'

He rose and the Inspector followed suit. 'What do you think, Watson?' he enquired as he returned from escorting the policeman to the door.

'I think you exaggerate the man's importance,' I said. 'The newspaper makes clear that he is merely a religious maniac. All that babbling about Ashtaroth and Mary, Herod and John! Clearly a lunatic!'

'Lunacy', said Holmes, 'is not bereft of logic. The maniac simply abandons the logic of our world and imposes his own system. Were it merely a question of Mary and John and Herod, I might well agree with you, but Ashtaroth and Sohrab do not belong in his fantasies.'

'Perhaps the reporter misheard him,' I suggested.

'Perhaps,' he replied. 'Watson, be a good fellow and ring for our luncheon.'

2

A DRAMATIC CLIENT

I was not greatly impressed by Lestrade's tale. I felt that his new duties bored and irked him and that he was making a great deal out of a trifling incident involving an evident madman, perhaps in the hope of embarking upon some trail of enquiries that would release him from his attendance upon foreign dignitaries. I was rather surprised to see that Holmes seemed to take the matter much more seriously.

After luncheon he cut the news report from the paper and took himself to the couch with that clipping, an encyclopaedia and a dictionary. He smoked so many pipes of shag that by late afternoon I was driven to take a stroll in the park for my lungs' sake.

He was still distant and abstracted after dinner and ignored my attempts at conversation so that I decided to retire early and leave him to his thoughts. It did occur to me, however, that I had a thousand times rather that he should spend his time with Lestrade's problem, be it ever so trivial, than reach out for the cocaine bottle.

Holmes startled me by being before me at breakfast in the morning, not his usual practice when he had no enquiry on hand. By the time I joined him he had made his daily analysis of the morning papers, which lay tumbled on the floor beside the table.

As I poured myself a cup of tea I reached down for a newspaper.

'There is little point, Watson,' Holmes remarked. 'Both the serious prints and the cheap papers are devoted almost entirely to the forthcoming Jubilee. Even the Radical papers manage to fill most of their pages with condemnations of the royal family, the Queen, the Court, the folly of the celebration, the unnecessary expense and any other complaint that occurs to them.'

'I was', I said, 'about to have a look at the sporting pages.'

'Ah!' said Holmes. 'I had forgotten to take account of your speciality, Watson. Perhaps while you examine them you would be kind enough to keep an eye on the entertainment columns.'

'Oh, if you fancy a theatre or a concert,' I said, 'there is no end of a choice in town at present.'

'I was wondering rather,' he said, 'if Lestrade's madman had made any further appearances.'

I worked my way through the sporting and theatrical pages as I ate my breakfast, discovering only that my racing selections of the previous day had all been unsuccessful.

'All of the newspapers', I remarked, 'seem to be devoting a great many words to the arrival of Colonel Cody's Wild West Show at the American Exhibition in Kensington. They have only been there for a few days, but half of fashionable London seems to have visited them.'

Holmes smiled. 'And we must do so, too,' he said. 'It will be a great pleasure to meet Cody again. He is truly one of the most singular men of this century.'

I had not been aware that my friend was acquainted with the American impresario, but I admit that the news items had intrigued me and I looked forward to visiting Cody's display.

'It seems', I said, when I had completed my review, 'that Inspector Lestrade has scared his lunatic away from theatres. Perhaps he will turn up somewhere else. Once their madness reaches a certain state these people seek any opportunity to display their disordered theories and beliefs.'

'Yes,' said Holmes, thoughtfully, 'and this particular madman seems to embrace theories that are more disordered than most.'

He did not choose to explain his remark and I was merely surprised again that he was still paying attention to Lestrade's tale.

Mrs Hudson had cleared the breakfast table and we sat smoking our pipes when the downstairs bell tinkled. Very shortly Mrs Hudson reappeared, handing Holmes a card.

He passed it to me as he told our landlady to show the visitor up. The card was that of 'John W. Byron, Dramatist' with an address in Bloomsbury.

'We seem', remarked my friend, 'to be drawn into theatrical themes, Watson.'

The door opened and Mrs Hudson ushered in our visitor. As soon as he rounded the door I was struck with astonishment. There was no doubt that this was the man described to us by Lestrade on the previous day. There could not be two such men in London.

I saw Holmes' eyes glint briefly as he took in the stranger's appearance and dress, but he gave no sign of surprise.

'Come in, Mr Byron,' he said warmly. 'Pray take the basket chair, I believe you will find it the more comfortable.'

Our flamboyant guest settled in the chair, spreading his cloak carefully about him and leaning his tall cane against the fireplace. I noted that, as Lestrade had described, our visitor's complexion had that distinctive, yellowish tinge which is so often the enduring mark borne by those whose health has been damaged by living in tropical climates.

'Do you smoke, Mr Byron?' asked Holmes. 'A cheroot perhaps, or a fill for your pipe?' and he indicated the Persian slipper.

'You are very kind, Mr Holmes,' said our client, 'but I will, if I may, stick to my own cigars.' He drew out an ornate silver case and extracted a small cigar. Once it was lighted he settled back in his chair, his wide-brimmed hat held across his knees. His voice was the slightly exaggerated voice of an actor, with a trace of the North Country in it.

'Now,' said Holmes, 'how can we help you, Mr Byron?'

The stranger looked long at Holmes, then said, 'They say, Mr Holmes, that you are the best detective in London, if not in the country.'

'Do they indeed?' said Holmes, 'and who says so, Mr Byron?'

'In my hearing, persons in the theatrical profession, Mr Holmes. What matters to me is whether their opinion is true.'

My friend smiled, warmed as always to hear that he was appreciated. 'I am not, perhaps, the source of which you should enquire. I can only tell you that my methods are my own and that they have brought me a certain amount of success.'

Again the stranger looked at Holmes contemplatively. 'I guess I must take my colleagues' opinion of you, Mr Holmes, for I am in great need of assistance.'

'You are of course a dramatist yourself,' remarked Holmes, 'though I confess I do not recognise your name. Do you use a *nom de plume*?'

Byron shook his silver locks. 'No, Mr Holmes,' he said, 'but there is no reason why you should know my name. My small efforts are staged in the provinces mainly, or in the less well-known houses in London. They provide a meagre living, but sufficient for my small needs.'

He fell silent, seemingly unwilling to broach the purpose of his visit, despite his claim of great need.

'You are not, I think, a Londoner by birth?' prompted Holmes.

'No, sir. I was born in Sheffield, where my father was a theatrical manager. As a child I saw the cream of the profession and it became my dearest wish to take to the boards. As a youth I tried the adventure, but it was not to be. Regretfully I was forced to take my father's advice and enter the Indian Service. I was fifteen years in India, Mr Holmes. I became an Assistant Collector, but the country was very nearly the death of me. My health suffered so that I was forced to resign my post and return to England, with only a small pension to support me.'

He shook his head again. 'Then the dreams of my youth returned to me. I determined that if I could not tread the boards I could, at least, pen a passable drama or melodrama, romance or comedy. So I have supported myself for a good few years now. I am not, as I have said, among the leading lights of my profession, Mr Holmes, but there are a number of managers in London and about the country who know my work and that I am reliable. That is all my story, Mr Holmes.'

'But it is not', said Holmes, 'your problem.'

'No, sir. That is so strange a thing that it might have come from one of my own melodramas.'

He paused and for a moment I thought that he was going to shy again at telling us of his problem, but he drew a long breath and continued.

'I live', he said, 'simply, as you may imagine. When I am not at home I am usually to be found at the British Museum. Occasionally I go to the theatre, sometimes to see my own plays, sometimes to see the work of others. Outside the world of the theatre I have no particular friends nor, so far as I know, any particular enemies. Nevertheless, Mr Holmes, in recent weeks I have come to feel threatened.'

'Threatened?' repeated Holmes. 'In what way?'

'I am followed, Mr Holmes.'

'By whom?' demanded my friend.

'I do not know, Mr Holmes. I have told you – I have no enemies that I know of, but the pattern is so persistent that I cannot be imagining it. I am followed – and I can only opine that some harm is meant to me.'

'A pattern!' exclaimed Holmes. 'What is the pattern, Mr Byron?'

'If I venture out during the day, say to the Museum, there are two men who dog my footsteps, though not always together. Both seem, by their dress, to be sailors. One is a tall man with greying hair, somewhat into middle age. The other is shorter and of a stocky build, with fair hair, perhaps in his late twenties.'

'And why do you believe that they follow you?'

'Mr Holmes, they do not merely follow me to the Museum, but one or another, usually the elder, follows me to the Reading Room. He sits as long as I do and purports to make notes, but actually he keeps observation on me.'

'And what', asked Holmes, 'do you do in the Reading Room of the British Museum that is worth observing?'

'Nothing!' exclaimed Byron. 'I go there to read history in the hope of discovering incidents that I can use in my little dramas. I often spend whole days sitting at a desk with one or two books on some forgotten aspect of history.'

'There is nothing in your researches which might, in any way at all, threaten anyone?'

'I cannot imagine it, Mr Holmes. My plays are set in past centuries, back to the Middle Ages, and often in remote places. What could I put on the stage that would cause any living person concern? Besides, my sources are books available to anyone upon the shelves of the Museum.'

'True,' said Holmes, and steepled his long fingers in front of his face. 'Tell me,' he continued, 'do these two men follow you to places other than the Museum?'

'Surely,' said Byron, with some warmth. 'In the evenings I have only to take a stroll around the square to find one of them at my back. When I visit theatres, they follow my cab in another. When I leave a theatre, they will be waiting outside. On occasions when I have taken supper with a theatrical colleague I have seen them loitering outside the restaurant.'

'You seem pretty well acquainted with their habits, Mr Byron. Is that because they take no trouble to conceal themselves?'

'I became aware of them several weeks ago, when the evenings were darker. At first I was not certain that they were following me, but their persistence and the lighter evenings have given me ample opportunity to confirm my suspicions.'

'Why do you fear that they mean you harm?'

'What else can be their purpose, Mr Holmes? I refuse to be frightened by them, but I am an old man and my health is not of the best. Some years since I broke an ankle which still troubles me. I cannot try conclusions with two stronger men in the street, Mr Holmes. I must drive them off somehow. That is why I have brought my problem to you.'

'What have the official police told you?' asked Holmes.

Byron avoided Holmes' eyes. 'I have not consulted them,' he admitted. 'I am not convinced that they would take this matter seriously. I can point to no actual harm, nor even any explicit threat. I need to be assured that whatever these men plan is frustrated. I asked among my theatrical friends for the name of a private agent of skill and determination and your name was given to me several times, so I opined that I must lay the matter before you. Can you help me, Mr Holmes? Will you help me?'

'I can relieve your mind a little straightaway,' replied my friend. 'You need not, I think, fear harm at the hands of these men. Had that been their intention, they have had numerous opportunities. No – they are about something else. I admit that I cannot, at present, understand their purpose, but I shall do, Mr Byron, I shall do.'

He rose and handed our visitor his long cane. 'You must go about your business as usual, Mr Byron. Do not vary your movements in any particular. In that way I shall have the opportunity to watch the watchers and we shall see what emerges.'

21

Byron rose heavily from the basket chair. 'And you really believe that I am in no danger?'

'You have my assurance on that point, Mr Byron.'

'Then I am mightily obliged to you, Mr Holmes. I am not a wealthy man, but I will pay any reasonable price to rid myself of these followers.'

'You will not find me unreasonable,' said Holmes. 'Now, back to Bloomsbury and continue your play-writing, Mr Byron!'

As he closed the door behind the dramatist Holmes was smiling broadly and, as he returned to his chair, he rubbed his hands with pleasure.

'Well, Watson,' he said. 'What do you make of our good fortune?'

'I do not see that it is good fortune,' I said. 'I saw that you had recognised Byron as the man that Lestrade described to us, but what of it?'

'What of it, Watson?' he repeated. 'Why! Lestrade's strange little mystery has begun to unfold like a flower. Now it is up to me to play the bee and see what honey I may extract.'

'Holmes,' I said, 'everything that he told you might have been the delusion of a madman.'

'Ho, so you still think him mad, Watson?'

'It is well known that certain kinds of lunatic evince obsessions that they are being hounded, followed, threatened or persecuted. I recall a fellow in Afghanistan, a corporal who became entirely convinced that the cook was putting drugs in his food. No one was minded to take him very seriously until he tried to shoot the wretched cook.'

'Did you observe any signs of madness in him, Watson?' countered Holmes.

'Well, no. But again, they may not emerge until some tiny thing triggers them off. Why did you not ask him about his behaviour at the theatre?'

'If he is indeed mad,' said Holmes, 'or if he knows how to feign insanity, he would have delivered a mouthful of religious gibberish, declared me to be one of the enemies of his faith, and stalked out. On the other hand, if he is sane, then he has what he conceives to be good reason for not mentioning that episode to me. Had I referred to it, he would have claimed mistaken identity or offered some untrue explanation. I am not here to be lied to by my own clients, Watson, and Mr Byron has told me a number of lies today.'

'In that case,' I said, 'I am the more surprised that you so readily accepted him as a client.'

'Lestrade's little story has aroused my curiosity, Watson. Mr Byron can either tell me the answer or, if he does not himself know it, lead me to it.'

'Then you believe in his mysterious followers?'

'Despite your medical advice, Watson, I do.'

3

GRANDMOTHER'S FOOTSTEPS

Nothing lightened my friend's mood so much as the belief that a new enquiry was making progress. At the same time it had a marked effect upon his appetite. Holmes ate heartily at luncheon, chatting the while about Anglo-Saxon kingship, the phonograph and many other topics. It was I who drew him back to our peculiar client.

'Why do you say he lied to you this morning?' I asked.

'It is possible', he replied, 'that the only truths he told us were that he was being followed, that he had once been an actor and that he had injured his ankle, though even those may have been untruths like everything else he said.'

'Everything!' I exclaimed.

'Everything,' confirmed Holmes. 'Start from the name, Watson.'

'It is unusual,' I agreed, 'but so is your own first name and my second.'

'First and second names, Watson, are bestowed at the whim of doting or pretentious parents. Surnames are either inherited or adopted. Byron as a surname is extremely rare, and the more remarkable that our client claims no kinship with the playwright J.H. Byron, whose name is well known and who is only recently deceased.'

'He might have claimed the kinship of the poet,' I said.

'So he might, Watson, though the poet's own name was the far less romantic George Gordon. Lord Byron was his title. There was also Mr Byron's ring.'

'His ring?' I said.

'Really, Watson! Do you observe nothing when a man sits two yards from you and delivers himself of a strange story? He wore a large ring on his left hand. It was of good gold, but had no jewel. Instead it was surmounted by an enamelled plaque, bearing a design which appeared to consist of his initials contained within a circlet of gold. If he cannot readily remove that ring he must be restricted in the aliases which he can adopt.'

'But he was an actor,' I said.

'So it appears from his voice, mannerisms and dress. As to the voice, what did you make of it, Watson?'

'I thought he spoke like an actor, but there was a trace of Yorkshire about it. Still, he did say that he was born in Sheffield.'

'He may have been,' conceded Holmes, 'but there were other aspects of his speech that I found strange. One would have expected an actor to seek to eliminate that trace of Yorkshire, but I formed the distinct impression that at times he emphasised it, perhaps to support his story.'

I nodded and he went on.

'Now his complexion reveals that he has indeed spent time in some tropical country and has suffered the consequences, but his speech does not suggest India.'

'What does it suggest?' I asked.

'Did you not note his use of "surely" where an Englishman would have said "certainly", his "mightily" rather than "greatly"? Most particularly, he used the word "opined", a perfectly respectable old English word, for which there is, indeed, no synonym, but one that seems to have become exclusively American.'

'You believe him to be an American?'

'If he is not, then he has certainly spent many years in that country, so that he is unable entirely to eliminate its usages from his speech. Remember also that it was an American at whom he aimed his attack at the theatre.'

'And despite these untruths and concealments you still believe in his tale of followers?'

'Of course, Watson. He knows that I shall investigate that matter. He has not invented them.'

'And how will you investigate?' I enquired.

'By watching the watchers, of course.'

He disappeared from Baker Street that afternoon, vanishing whilst I was out. For four days and nights I saw nothing of him, and could only surmise that he was about his enquiries.

25

I returned one afternoon from playing billiards with my friend Thurston and found that I was a little before my time for tea.

I had settled myself comfortably with a new magazine when Mrs Hudson appeared, rather earlier than I had expected, and ushered into the sitting-room a tall, ill-dressed individual.

'Dr Watson,' she said, 'this is a Mr Carter, a painter and decorator. It seems that Mr Holmes has summoned him to meet with him and most particularly wished that he should wait here. I hope it does not inconvenience you.'

If it was Holmes' arrangement I could do no other than acquiesce, but I admit that I was not pleased to have my quiet reading disturbed by this individual. He took the seat I indicated and sat, staring round him. He was a man of middle years, pallid of face with the pallor that comes in painters from the use of poisonous materials. His mouth was entirely concealed by a thick, tobacco-stained moustache and an unkempt beard fringed his jaw. His tattered clothing was liberally stained with variegated paint splashes and even across the width of the room it was impossible to ignore the strong odour of turpentine that emanated from him.

I had returned to my magazine when my companion enquired, 'This Mr Holmes, governor – will he be very long?'

'I have not the least idea,' I said. 'If he has sent for you to meet him here, then I imagine that he will soon be here.'

His eyes wandered about the room again, falling upon the area of plaster pock-marked by Holmes' indoor pistol practice.

'That's remarkable uncommon,' he said. 'Them marks on your wall looks exactly like the letters V and R, almost as if they was a Jubilee decoration.'

'They are not,' I replied, shortly. 'They have been there some time.' I was not about to discuss my friend's eccentricities with this intruder.

It was at this point that Mrs Hudson reappeared. 'I know that Mr Holmes has not returned, Doctor, but I wondered if I should serve your tea now.'

I had no intention of taking my refreshment in an atmosphere of turpentine and was about to say so when a familiar voice said, 'If you will allow me a few minutes to change my clothing,

Mrs Hudson, there is nothing I would find more welcome than a cup of tea.'

'Holmes!' I cried, and Mrs Hudson clapped her hands and laughed aloud. 'Mr Holmes,' she said, 'I often wonder that you are not on the stage. I shall bring your tea in a quarter of an hour.'

Holmes, for it was indeed he, sat pulling tufts of hair from his face and flinging them into the waste-paper basket. 'Why', I grumbled, 'do I always fail to detect your impersonations?'

'Ah, Watson,' he said, 'you are not the only one who has been deceived by Mr Carter. He has been of great assistance to me in my enquiries. A pot of paint in the hand clearly indicates that one is a craftsman bent about some task in the neighbourhood and a strong odour of turpentine discourages any close examination.'

He uncoiled himself from the armchair. 'Now, I must restore myself a little before we take tea.'

Within minutes we were at the tea-table and I noted that my friend's eyes glittered, the false pallor of the painter had vanished and his appetite was hearty.

'You have, then, enjoyed some success in the matter of Mr Byron?' I suggested.

'Oh, indeed,' he confirmed. 'I have passed a thoroughly enjoyable time pursuing Mr Byron about London, and I have made a number of interesting discoveries.'

'Such as?' I prompted.

'It is the case that our client is regularly followed by two such men as he described, either singly or as a pair, but they are not the only persons on his track.'

'They are part of a larger gang?' I suggested.

'I think not, Watson, for they seem to be unaware that they, in their turn, are followed.'

'Two sets of watchers!' I exclaimed. 'That is extraordinary.'

'So it is, Watson. So it is. But there is more. Our playwright has gone about his business for these last few days at the head of a convoy that has been, at times, longer than the procession which will accompany Her Majesty to the Abbey for her Jubilee. Can you imagine, Watson, that our client is sometimes followed by no fewer than seven individuals?'

27

'Seven!' I cried. 'But that is impossible! Why did he only refer to two? Surely he cannot be unaware of the others.'

'Ah, but he is, Watson, for there is an advantage in being part of this strange train. The second party needs only to watch the movements of the first, and the third of the second. On occasions when the procession was complete I have had the advantage of being able to remain completely out of Mr Byron's sight.'

I shook my head in wonderment, while Holmes buttered a tea-cake. 'But who', I asked, 'are all these people and what on earth is their interest in Byron?'

'The first pair are as they were described to us. They are the most persistent. They take turn and turn about at watching Byron's home and fall in behind whenever he ventures out. They, I believe, are the paid agents of some other party.'

'And what of the second pair?' I enquired.

'Like the first, they are not always a pair. Sometimes it is only one man, an individual as singular in his way as our client. He is a tall man who wears a wide-brimmed grey hat, sports a wide moustache, dresses in a braided blue coat that suggests a uniform and is sometimes accompanied by a greyhound. His, I suspect, is a personal interest, for I cannot imagine that anyone would employ a man of such memorable appearance to follow someone. His occasional companion is a youth of more conventional appearance, a well-built young man with long, fair hair.'

'And you say that Byron has not, apparently, spotted this memorable individual?'

'No, Watson. I am sure of that. However, the man in the braided coat seems only to pursue Byron in the evenings. His forays to the Museum are accompanied only by the two sailors, and because of their invariable presence at Byron's heels, the moustached gentleman hangs back and is rarely within Byron's sight.'

'And the third party?' I said.

'Oh, they are readily identifiable,' said Holmes. 'Unless I miss my mark, they are Scotland Yarders.'

'Scotland Yarders!' I repeated. 'But you advised Lestrade not to have Byron followed.'

'So I did, and for once I believe that he has heeded my advice. The third pair are, I believe, two of Littlechild's men from the Fenian Branch at the Yard.'

'And what do you surmise is going on?'

'I may be theorising too far ahead of my data, Watson, but it occurs to me that, so far from posing a threat to Byron, the first pair have been assigned to protect him.'

'From what?' I asked.

'Why, from the second pair, one imagines. Their purposes I cannot, at present, determine, but it is the moustached gentleman who interests Littlechild, for his men are only present when the man in the braided coat appears.'

He rose from the table and, seating himself at the writing-desk, began to pen a note.

When he had finished, I asked, 'How will you proceed now?'

'I have left the Baker Street Irregulars to form the rear of Mr Byron's procession. A day or two more of Mr Carter and he might have been noticed, even by Littlechild's operatives, but a covey of street urchins will pass unremarked anywhere in London. In the meantime I propose to take advantage of Scotland Yard's greater resources to acquire some necessary data.'

4

THE RESOURCES OF SCOTLAND YARD

As Holmes and I finished our breakfast the next morning he asked Mrs Hudson to bring us another pot of tea and an extra cup and saucer, saying, 'We shall have a visitor shortly.'

'Heavens, Holmes!' I exclaimed. 'Have you become clairvoyant?'

'Not at all, Watson. I am merely positive that our friend Lestrade will be here as soon as he has made certain enquiries at the Yard.'

I do not recall that I ever heard Holmes make a prediction that was not soon fulfilled. Within the half-hour Mrs Hudson showed the Inspector in.

'Watson,' said Holmes, as the little detective settled himself in a chair, 'do pour the Inspector a cup of tea. You look rattled, Lestrade. You have hurried here.'

'I have indeed, Mr Holmes, and I am rattled. I have had a most uncomfortable interview with Mr Littlechild this morning.'

He drew from his coat pocket a letter, which I could see was in Holmes' writing, and cast his eyes over it as he drank his tea.

'That's better!' he exclaimed, placing his cup and saucer back on the table. 'That hit the spot.' He lifted the letter to Holmes. 'Might I ask why you wrote me this letter, Mr Holmes?'

'It is a simple request for information, Lestrade, aimed at discovering the identities of certain persons who have attracted my notice. I may criticise Scotland Yard's methods in certain matters, but I entirely applaud the Yard's accumulation of information about London's wrongdoers. Being a lone agent I am not able to maintain more than my index volumes, which will never be sufficiently detailed to be really useful.'

'In what connection have you come across these men, Mr Holmes?'

'Why, in one that you first drew to my attention only the other day.' Holmes went on to explain to Lestrade how Byron had called on us and the results of his observations.

'And you say that the third pair were two Scotland Yard men?' he said as Holmes' explanation ended.

'Indubitably,' confirmed Holmes.

Lestrade shook his head. 'I don't understand this at all,' he said. 'My association with you is well known at the Yard. It is, as a matter of fact, the subject of a certain amount of chaff. If there were officers watching these men and they observed you, they would have a word with me. Not to put too fine a point on it, they would have dropped a hint that I should warn you off, Mr Holmes.'

'If, as you rightly say, they had observed me,' said Holmes, sternly. 'When engaged in observation I do not make a practice of being noticed by anyone, Lestrade. Besides, they were not, I think, from your Division. They looked more like denizens of Littlechild's Fenian Branch.'

Lestrade nodded. 'They would be, Mr Holmes, they would be. But Mr Littlechild never said he was having the man followed.'

'Then the Yard does know something of these men?' said Holmes.

'Not all of them, no,' said the detective. 'The two sailors are not known to us, but the strange customer with the moustache is a big fish indeed.'

'Why do you say so?'

'When I got your letter this morning, Mr Holmes, I checked at once with our register of descriptions. I asked the sergeant who maintains it to search for the two sailors, which he did, and he assured me that he could find no such. However, in the meantime I had come across what was plainly a description of the moustached man, dated some long time ago. There was an entry in red ink alongside it, ordering that all information on this man should be passed at once to Mr Littlechild.'

He paused and Holmes smiled thinly.

'I asked the sergeant if the entry was still current and if the order in the margin still stood. "Oh yes," he said, "Mr Little-child has a very particular interest in that customer." So I did not dare keep the matter between us. I had to go and see Mr Littlechild.'

'And how did he respond?' asked Holmes.

'Well, Mr Holmes, I did not show him your letter, nor introduce your name into our discussion. I felt that only fair to you, sir. I explained that an informer had given me the description of a man who he believed was up to no good and that I had seen his order and presented myself.'

'Very fair of you, Lestrade,' said Holmes, expressionlessly.

'Well, he laughed, did Mr Littlechild. "Lestrade," he said, "that man has been up to no good for most of his lifetime, in this country, in America, Canada and on the Continent. Take it from me," he said, "that man is the vilest criminal walking the streets of this or any other city, but I have my eye on him and I shall lay him by the heels."'

I saw Holmes' eyes glint at the mention of America, but he remained silent. Inspector Lestrade went on.

'Then he looks at me sharply and "Who's your informer, Lestrade? How does he know this man?" he says. Well, Mr Holmes, that took me somewhat aback. I'm sure you understand that there are places at the Yard where it does no good to mention your name, and the Secret Branch I have always found hostile to you.'

'So what did you tell him?' asked Holmes.

'Well, sir, I had to pluck myself up and say to him that my informer had only said that he believed the man was engaged in some criminal enterprise and that I knew no more. All of which, of course, was strictly true. Then I put it to him, as one policeman to another, that the relationship between a nark and an officer is a fragile one that has to be based on trust and that I could not see my way clear to give him the name of my informer.'

'Bravo, Lestrade!' cried Holmes. 'And did he take it?'

'Quite well, Mr Holmes. He simmered down a bit and said, "Very well, Lestrade. You are assigned to me at present, so you're entitled to know something of this man. He has been coming and going from London and Liverpool for twenty years, always upon nefarious business. He has considerable funds at his disposal and his presence here at this time is because he intends to foment some outrage on behalf of the Fenian Brotherhood. He will attempt to mar Her Majesty's

32

Jubilee with some act that, if it succeeds, will damage Her Majesty and this nation in the eyes of the whole world. He is not to be watched, Lestrade, but any further information is to come to me without delay. As to your nark, you may promise him what rewards you think fit for news of our man. He must be stopped at all costs!" '

'I am gratified', interrupted Holmes, 'to hear that the Fenian Branch's Informers' Fund is to meet my costs in this matter,' and he smiled thinly.

Lestrade looked abashed, but he continued. 'Then Mr Little-child unlocked a drawer of his desk and took out a folder. He passed me some sheets of paper and said, "There, Lestrade, read all about your man." I asked if I might make notes, but he refused. However, as soon as he dismissed me I went straight to my own room and made my notes from memory.'

He pulled out his pocket-book, but Holmes laid a hand on his arm, saying, 'Watson, be a good fellow and ring for Mrs Hudson. I think that more tea would be welcome.'

Once we were refreshed the little detective addressed himself once more to his notes.

'His name', he announced, 'is Dr Francis J. Tumbletye. He claims to have been born in Dublin in 1833, but it appears that he may have been born in Canada. His family moved from Canada to Rochester in the United States and he spent his youth there. Although his early circumstances were poor, it seems that he supported himself by peddling indecent prints to travellers. He soon established himself in America as an "Indian Herbal Doctor", advertising all manner of remedies. If he ever studied medicine, it is not known where, though he has claimed a qualification from the Medical School at Dublin. He travelled widely in America and apparently made a very good thing of his quackery, amassing a considerable fortune. During the Civil War in America he spent a great deal of his time in Washington, where there is no doubt that he had access to numbers of prominent people, including, it is thought, President Lincoln himself. Although he affected exaggerated uniforms, he never took any part in the war, but he is said to have been attached to General Maclellan's staff. Throughout his life he has employed aliases, and under one such – Dr J. H. Blackburn

– he was arrested and held in custody as a suspect in the assassination of President Lincoln, though he was eventually released.'

'What of his connection with Britain?' asked Holmes, as Lestrade paused for a mouthful of tea.

'He has relatives in Ireland and in England, Mr Holmes, and for the last twenty years or so he has come and gone from England regularly, as well as travelling on the Continent. During these journeys he continues to present himself as a herbal doctor or an "electric doctor".'

'Quack doctors', interrupted Holmes, 'are ten a penny. Their activities may be undesirable, but they hardly represent the degree of criminality to which Littlechild referred.'

'Well, no, sir,' said the Inspector. 'It is Mr Littlechild's belief that Tumbletye comes to England on behalf of the Irish-American Fenians, that he supplies the movement in England with funds and devises their major schemes. He is widely known in America as a Fenian sympathiser and speaks in public for the Irish cause.'

'Which does not explain Littlechild's attitude to him,' said Holmes. 'By your account he twice referred to Tumbletye as "vile". Do you know why he applied that particular epithet?'

An expression of embarrassment clouded the Inspector's - sallow features. 'I think', he said, 'that Mr Littlechild's opinions are coloured by what is known of the suspect's personal life and habits.'

'They must be extraordinary in a high degree to sway the emotions of an officer of Littlechild's experience,' remarked Holmes.

Lestrade moved uncomfortably in his chair. 'Tumbletye is, how shall I say, a man of disgusting private habits, Mr Holmes. He is, er, sexually depraved. Although we understand him to have married in his youth and been widowed, he engages in the most revolting practices with young men. This is not mere suspicion,' he continued hurriedly. 'In America he went to law against the mother of a youth that he had employed as a secretary. He claimed that the boy had illegally disposed of some railway stocks and sought a large sum in compensation from the boy's mother. The youth entered a counterclaim, declaring that he had been the victim of outrageous assaults by Tumbletye, and the matter went no further.'

'Not', said Holmes, 'very impressive evidence. The testimony of a young man who may have been detected in serious financial defalcations.'

'It is, apparently, well known among Tumbletye's acquaintances that he eschews the company of women – indeed, he speaks most harshly of their moral character – and he is rarely without some good-looking young man as a companion or secretary,' said the Inspector.

'Despite the Labouchere Amendment,' said Holmes, 'the Doctor's private conduct is hardly a matter of great moment to Scotland Yard. What matters is Littlechild's belief that the man has significant involvement with the Fenians in this country.'

'The American connection is one which has been apparent in a number of Fenian cases,' said Lestrade. 'There was Lomasney, for example.'

'Quite,' said Holmes. 'The Fenian Brotherhood was, after all, founded in America and has long supplied assistance as well as money on this side of the Atlantic. There was Kelly in the Irish rising of 1867 and O'Sullivan Burke. Of much more interest to me is whether Littlechild knows of any connection between Tumbletye and Mr Byron.'

Lestrade shook his head. 'He mentioned none,' he said. 'I took your advice, Mr Holmes, and did not have Byron watched, but I have made certain enquiries. To all intents and purposes he seems to be as he described himself to you – a former Indian Civil Servant who retired early through ill health and now earns a modest living as a writer of melodramas and comedies.'

'Then your enquiries have not been pursued far enough, Lestrade,' said Holmes. 'A glance through the Green Book would have revealed to you, as it did to me, that no Collector or Assistant Collector, indeed no Civil Servant of any rank, of the name John W. Byron has been employed in India throughout the past several decades. Whoever and whatever Mr Byron may be, he is definitely not what he claims to be.'

'How do you think I should proceed then, Mr Holmes?' asked the Inspector. 'You seem to have made a connection between Tumbletye and Byron and that makes me suspect that Byron's behaviour at the theatre may have been part of some Fenian plot.'

'You may be right,' said Holmes. 'I can only suggest that you follow Mr Littlechild's instructions. In the meantime I, as your paid informer, will see that anything I discover about the American Doctor is made known to you.'

Lestrade thanked him warmly and left. Once again, as Holmes returned from the door he was smiling broadly. 'Well, Watson,' he enquired, 'what do you make of your Irish-American colleague?'

'Hardly a colleague,' I complained.

'No, perhaps not. But you must admit, Watson, that I seem to have started a very peculiar bird and not just in respect of its extraordinary plumage!'

He was in high good humour for the remainder of the day, sometimes taking out the newspaper account of Byron's attack on the American businessman and poring over it.

With our tea, Mrs Hudson brought in a small and grubby boy whom I recognised as one of Holmes' 'Baker Street Irregulars' – the corps of street arabs who were his eyes and ears when he was not himself about the metropolis.

'I'm sorry, Mr Holmes,' apologised our landlady, 'I tried to have him wait downstairs, but he insisted on delivering his message in person.'

The boy reached inside his tattered jacket and produced a soiled and folded paper which he handed to Holmes. My friend read it with a smile and passed it to me while he rewarded the courier with a coin. In a second he was gone, his battered boots thudding down our seventeen stairs.

The paper was written in a clumsy scrawl, but its message was clear:

The sailers has gorn. They was on the job
larst nihgt but they are gorn this mornin.
                        Yours fathfully,
                        H. Wiggins
                        Captain of Ireglars.

'What', said Holmes, when I had read it, 'do you imagine that means?'

I admitted that I had no idea. 'At the very least,' he said, thoughtfully, 'it seems to point to some new development.'

5

A DEAD MAN'S HAND

We did not have to wait long for an answer to Holmes' question. A wire from Lestrade sent us to Wapping Mortuary as soon as we had broken our fast.

The Inspector met us there, his hands thrust deep in his coat pockets and his collar turned up against an unseasonably brisk wind along the river.

'Good morning, Mr Holmes, Doctor!' he greeted us. 'Sorry to bring you here on a day like this, but when I came on duty this morning I found a fresh description posted and it seems like one of your men.'

He led us into the mortuary and brought us to a slab where the corpse of a fair-haired young man lay. Holmes took a brief glance and turned to Lestrade.

'This', he said, 'is the younger of the two sailors. Where was he found?'

'The River Police spotted him about three o'clock this morning,' replied Lestrade. 'He was lying half in and half out of the water just along the river at Cuckolds' Point.'

Holmes turned back to the cadaver and examined it closely. When he had done, he invited my opinion as to the cause of death.

'He was first bludgeoned, from behind,' I said, when I had completed my own examination, 'then stabbed directly into the heart with what seems to have been a long, thin-bladed weapon.'

Holmes nodded his agreement, but Lestrade asked, 'Could the head injury have happened after death, Doctor? We usually find that dead men out of the river has been struck by a boat or run into a river pier. Dreadful mess some of them is in.'

'I don't believe so,' I replied. 'The mark is round and even, with no surface abrasion. It seems to me that he was struck one forceful blow with something heavy like a life preserver, a sap or something of that kind.'

'How long do you think he's been dead, Doctor?' asked the detective. 'We used to be able to tell by the fleas, you know, but people are getting more pernickety, even sailors. We couldn't find any on him.'

'It is difficult to say,' I said. 'The weather is chilly, the water will be cold, so it is not surprising that the body is cold. He is not stiff, which suggests that he has been dead half a day or longer, but rigor mortis is unreliable. Sometimes it fails to manifest and sometimes it sets in and passes off very rapidly.'

'The river, as you say, Lestrade, is busy night and day. Unless he was flung in very close to here, the absence of injuries from flotsam, vessels or bridges suggests that he was not long in the Thames,' remarked Holmes. 'Where are his clothes?'

Lestrade called an attendant and sent him for the clothing. He returned shortly with a sodden bundle which Holmes examined minutely.

'Cheap sailors' clothing, probably from the slop shops on the Ratcliffe Highway,' he said. 'No distinguishing features or marks. Was there anything in his pockets?'

Lestrade showed us a number of items laid out on a table. 'The sheath knife was on his belt, at the back,' he said. 'The clasp knife and tobacco were in the right-hand pocket of his smock, together with the box of vestas. The three cards are all for houses in Rosemary Lane and the Highway. There was nothing else apart from the few coins.'

Holmes picked up the damp twist of black tobacco and sniffed at it. 'American,' he said, and dropped it back on the table. 'Have the girls at the three houses been questioned?'

'They have,' said Lestrade, 'and have been about as helpful as girls of that type usually are. Two of them recognised his description, but said they knew him only as "Dick" and they hadn't seen him for weeks.'

'Could they confirm that he was an American?'

'They did think he was a Yankee, yes.'

'Then we have two certain facts,' said Holmes, 'that he was American and a sailor.'

39

'From the tobacco and the girls?' said Lestrade. 'I suppose so, but American tobacco is common and you can't trust whores.'

Holmes turned back to the slab and took the corpse by a big toe. 'In identifying our man as American,' he said, 'I was relying rather upon this than upon the word of an East End doxy,' and he pointed to the sole of the foot.

'Good heavens!' I exclaimed, for the dead man's foot bore a clear tattoo of a rabbit. 'What does that signify, Holmes?'

'That he was a sailor and an American,' said Holmes. 'I believe it is only American sailors who regard such a tattoo as a protection against drowning. Our own mariners prefer to carry a baby's caul for the same purpose. Come, Watson, I think there is nothing more to be learned here.'

We were leaving the mortuary with the Inspector when a uniformed constable saluted Lestrade. 'Beg pardon, sir,' he said, 'but I thought you would wish to know that the River Police are bringing another stiff ashore now.'

We hurried to the foreshore with Lestrade. A River Police launch lay at the jetty and we could see that the dead man being brought ashore was dressed in a very similar fashion to the corpse we had just examined.

The cadaver was stripped and laid out while the River Police officers gave Holmes and Lestrade an account of finding it in the water, close to Cuckolds' Point. Holmes and I cast our eyes over it. I was particularly careful to note the soles of the feet on this occasion, but found no rabbit nor any other tattoo. The remains were those of a stocky man of about forty-five, with dark, greying hair. There were old, faded injury scars on his left thigh, but it was at once apparent to both Holmes and me that this man had met his death in an identical fashion to the young American, having entirely similar injuries.

'Well, Mr Holmes?' queried Lestrade when we had done.

'This', said Holmes, 'is the second of the pair of watchers that I characterised as sailors, though unlike his American colleague this man has not been at sea for some time.'

'Are you sure?' said the Inspector.

Holmes turned up the palm of the dead man's right hand. 'Observe,' he commanded Lestrade. 'The callouses are old. The

40

younger man's hands are much more indicative of recent hand-
ling of ropes. Have you searched his clothing yet?'

'Yes, Mr Holmes,' said Lestrade, and led us over to the table
where a second display had joined the first. 'No sheath knife, no
clasp knife,' he recited. 'Box of cigarettes in left-hand smock
pocket with box of vestas, one sovereign and small change,
pocket life-preserver in right-hand trouser pocket and this in
the shirt pocket,' and he picked up two sheets of bedraggled
paper, folded together.

Holmes took the papers and spread them separately on the
table. They were handwritten in ink and seemed to be the pages
of a letter, but the Thames water had worked havoc on the ink,
so that little if anything of the text was still legible.

Drawing his lens from his coat pocket Holmes peered at the
sodden documents. 'Faugh!' he exclaimed after a while. 'There is
virtually nothing discernible here. I believe the hand to be that of
a woman. What do you make of that, Watson?' and he drew my
attention to a fragment of a word in the address which still
remained partly legible.

I took his lens and scanned the word. 'I cannot make out the
entire word,' I said. 'The first letters are lost, but I believe the
next few to be "o-n-c-e-s" or perhaps "o-u-c-e-s", though I
should have thought the latter unlikely.'

'There is certainly only one word of such length incorporating
that sequence of letters in common English usage,' agreed
Holmes, and turned to Lestrade. 'This man was wearing a signet
ring,' he said. 'Was it not possible to remove it?'

'No, sir,' said Lestrade. 'We might have better luck when the
flesh has dried out a bit.'

'No matter,' said Holmes, and carried his lens across to the
slab.

Turning the dead man's hand down, Holmes applied his lens
to the large gold ring which the man wore. After rubbing away
with his handkerchief a film of Thames dirt, he made a careful
examination then said, 'Watson, might I trouble you for a page
from your pocket-book?'

I supplied one and, taking out a pencil and reapplying his
lens, he made a quick drawing of the design enamelled on the
ring.

41

When he had done, he straightened up and tucked away the pencil and paper. 'Lestrade,' he said, 'I shall be grateful if you will have both the dead men photographed – their faces only – and more grateful if copies could be sent to Baker Street by this evening.'

The Inspector confirmed that it would be done and very shortly we were outside the mortuary once more.

'Watson,' said Holmes. 'I must leave you to return to Baker Street alone. I must pursue certain enquiries.'

6

MESSENGERS OF GRIEF

I had imagined that Holmes would now disappear back to
Bloomsbury, adopt his disguise as Carter the painter or some
other alternative, and leave me in ignorance of his whereabouts
for some time.

I was, therefore, the more surprised when he returned to
Baker Street before teatime. I had also expected that the mysterious murders of the two watchers might have sent him into one
of his periods of intense reflection while he sought some meaning in the killings, but was again surprised to find him cheerful
and with a hearty appetite.

After tea he sprawled on the couch smoking his pipe. 'Be a
good fellow, Watson,' he requested. 'Make a long arm and pass
me Bradshaw's. We must be on the way to Gloucestershire early
tomorrow.'

'Gloucestershire!' I exclaimed, as I passed him the timetable.
'Why are we going to Gloucestershire?'

He shook his head as he thumbed through Bradshaw. 'Not
only', he said, 'do you fail to consider the significance of what
you have observed, Watson, but you continue to misunderstand
when I have underlined the essential part of the observation.
One of our dead men had received a letter from a woman.'

'From Gloucestershire?' I asked.

'Watson, Watson,' he said. 'What other word is so long and
contains the sequence "o-u-c-e-s"?'

'But', I argued, 'you cannot be sure that the letter was written
to the dead man. It might even have been placed upon his body
to mislead any enquiry!'

'The dead men', he said, 'were despatched quickly and
expertly by a person or persons who knew exactly what they
were doing. Had such a person created a letter to mislead and
placed it in the older man's shirt, it would hardly have been

written with an ink that dissolved so completely in river water. Besides,' he added, 'it is not only the letter that indicates Gloucestershire.'

I was about to question him further, but he flung me the railway timetables and rose from the couch to pick up his violin. For an hour he was lost in his music and I was pleased that it was not one of those frustrated occasions when he merely repeated disconnected phrases and extemporised tuneless sequences of notes. Instead he played his own variations on well-known airs with great skill.

It was scarcely more than twenty-four hours since we had stood on the chilly banks of the Thames at Wapping watching a dead man being brought ashore when we found ourselves nearer to the river's source, on the platform of a country railway station. The weather had improved steadily as we travelled westwards and it was a warm, sunny May morning.

The station dogcart carried Holmes and me into a pretty little village, whose cottages, built of the local stone, were pale golden in the sunlight. Here and there old people sat in their colourful gardens, enjoying the May sunshine. There are few English counties which can match the scenes and scents of Gloucestershire in summer, and nothing can have been less like the cold, overcast Thames of the previous morning.

We passed through the length of the village and, a few hundred yards beyond the last cottage, turned in at a pair of ancient stone pillars. A screen of thick trees hid our destination from the road, but once inside the gates we could see that a short drive led through colourful gardens to the front of a handsome stone manor house, some three centuries old.

The dogcart stopped in front of the house, and Holmes leapt down, asking the driver to wait for us. As I climbed down I saw him smiling up at the coat of arms carved above the doorway.

The blackened oak door was opened at our ring by an elderly butler. Holmes presented his card and asked to see the lady of the house.

'That will be Mrs Tremaille, sir,' the elderly retainer replied. 'If you will be so kind as to wait, I shall inform Mrs Tremaille of your visit.'

He led us to a pleasant library, where the sun, striking through mullioned and leaded windows, fell upon shelves of ancient, leather-bound volumes. Holmes strode to a table where a number of framed photographs were displayed. After a moment he selected one and showed it to me. It was a picture of a youth in the uniform of a Royal Naval cadet.

'Who is he, Holmes?' I asked.

He passed me another. This one showed a young man in an unfamiliar naval uniform, standing at the rail of a vessel. The features were vaguely familiar, but I could not identify him.

I had handed the photograph back to my friend when the door opened to admit a tall young woman. She was dark-haired and dark-eyed and I saw at once that she resembled the young man in the photographs. Behind her the elderly butler pushed a tea-trolley.

'Good morning, gentlemen,' she said. 'I am Laura Tremaille. My mother apologises for not attending you, but she had not expected company this morning. She says that she will be done with her commitments in the garden very shortly. In the meantime, you have travelled from London and I am sure refreshment will be welcome.'

When we are all seated and tea served, Holmes remarked, 'Your mother's garden looks particularly lovely this morning.'

'It does, Mr Holmes,' she replied. 'Some prefer a garden in the height of its summer blooming, but I prefer it at this time. If the weather is kind in early May, the garden is never more attractive.'

'May I ask', said Holmes, 'if the handsome achievement of arms over your front door is that of your family?'

'Oh, indeed,' she said. 'The Tremailles built this house and it has always been ours. Those arms were put there by my ancestor who first occupied it.'

'I was looking', said Holmes, 'at your family photographs. I take it from his features that the young man in Royal Naval uniform is a Tremaille?'

A shadow seemed to flit across her face and she bent her head to her tea for a moment. Then she looked up, and there seemed to be a hint of defiance in her voice as she replied, 'Yes, Mr Holmes. That is my brother – Ashley Tremaille. He was a cadet in his youth.'

'Am I right in believing', asked Holmes, 'that the uniform worn by your brother in the later picture is not of the Royal Navy, but of the United States Navy?'

'No,' she said, sharply, 'you are not, Mr Holmes. I do not know what interest you have in my brother, but there is little to know about him. He was, as I stated, a cadet in the Royal Navy. Through boyish folly he was dismissed the Service over a matter of gambling debts. He felt that he had disgraced the family and was unable to face our late father. The next we heard of Ashley was from Canada. He remained in that country until the commencement of the war in America, when he was commissioned in the Navy of the Confederacy.'

She set down her cup and saucer, firmly, and her chin lifted.

'He served the Confederacy at sea,' she continued, 'until he was wounded in the latter part of 1863. Thereafter he was forced to serve his adopted country on land, but he did so until the end of hostilities. Since then he has made his home in America and visits us only infrequently. Does that satisfy your curiosity, Mr Holmes?'

'I do assure you, Miss Tremaille,' said Holmes, mildly, 'that my enquiries are not merely a matter of curiosity. Equally I would assure you that I mean no harm to your brother or to your family. Do you know the nature of your brother's employment for the Confederacy after he was wounded?'

Miss Tremaille scanned Holmes' face carefully before replying. Then she said, 'I believe he was employed in that country's Secret Service in Canada and in Bermuda. He spoke to me once of something called the "Golden Circle".'

'The Golden Circle,' repeated Holmes, and drew a deep breath. He was evidently about to ask a further question, but at that moment the door opened once more, to admit a tall lady in her sixties, who advanced into the room smiling broadly.

'Mr Holmes,' she said, 'I am so sorry to have kept you waiting, but I see that Laura has entertained you and seen to your refreshment.'

When we had been introduced she took a seat and looked at my friend expectantly.

'And what', she enquired, 'brings a consulting detective all the way from London to our little village, Mr Holmes?'

46

Before he could reply the younger woman forestalled him. 'Mr Holmes', she said, 'has been enquiring about Ashley, Mother. In particular about the work which he did for the Confederacy after he left their Navy.'

'Would you be so kind as to tell me why you are enquiring into my son's affairs, Mr Holmes?' said Mrs Tremaille, and her smile had vanished.

'I have already assured your daughter that I mean no harm to any member of your family,' said Holmes. 'I am engaged upon a commission for a private client in London and, in the course of my enquiries, I have come across a man who might well be your son. It is of the greatest importance that I should identify that man and discover what connection exists between him and my client.'

'Surely your client can explain that to you,' said Miss Tremaille.

Holmes shook his head. 'My client has, it seems, no knowledge of the man,' he said.

'If there is any such connection,' asserted the older woman, 'I am sure that it is a perfectly lawful and upright one. Ashley's one act of dishonour in his youth cost him dear and taught him the value of a sense of honour.'

'I do not doubt it,' said Holmes. 'Indeed, I had formed a belief that your son – if it is he – was protecting my client, but I need to know on whose behalf and against what danger he did so.'

'Why do you not simply ask Ashley?' said Miss Tremaille.

Holmes did not answer, but asked another question. 'Can you tell me, Mrs Tremaille, what your son has done since the end of the Civil War in America?'

'He was a loyal officer of the Confederacy,' she said, 'but when that unhappy nation ceased to exist, he took the oath of loyalty to the United States and has always lived by it. When his wounds were sufficiently healed he went back to sea and, from time to time, he has found occasion to visit us when his voyagings have brought him to England.'

'He has been in England very recently, has he not?' said Holmes, and when neither lady answered he continued, 'Did you not, Mrs Tremaille, write to him at an address in London recently?'

Mrs Tremaille shook her head, wonderingly. 'I see that it is of no use to attempt concealment from you, Mr Holmes. I do not know how you come by your knowledge, but you say that you mean no harm to my son.' She searched his impassive face with her eyes. 'I believe I must trust you, Mr Holmes. Yes, I have written to my son at an address in London. It was in care of Craig's Antiquarian Bookshop in the Charing Cross Road.'

'Thank you, Mrs Tremaille,' said Holmes, and noted the address in his pocket-book.

As he looked up from making the note she asked, 'Do you believe that Ashley is in danger, Mr Holmes?'

'I fear', said Holmes, gravely, 'that your son may already have come to harm,' and he took from his pocket one of the photographs supplied by Lestrade. 'I have no wish to distress you, Mrs Tremaille, but I must ask if this is a photograph of Ashley?'

She reached out and took the picture and, before she had drawn it to her, said, 'Yes, yes, that is Ashley.' Then, as she held the photograph in front of her, her features paled. 'But,' she stammered, 'he is dead!'

'I am afraid so, Mrs Tremaille,' said Holmes quietly.

Mrs Tremaille fell, sobbing, into her daughter's arms, and for several minutes the two wept together. At last the elder lady recovered herself a little and turned again to Holmes.

'You must forgive us, Mr Holmes,' she said. 'Can you tell us how Ashley met his end?'

'There is nothing to forgive,' replied my friend. 'The enterprise upon which your son was engaged was one that exposed him to desperate men. He and a young companion were attacked and killed two days ago.'

'And do you know the identity of the killer?' asked Laura Tremaille.

'No, Miss Tremaille, but I hope that the information which you and your mother have supplied will lead me to him.' He rose. 'I deeply regret that I have had to bring such distressing tidings,' he said, 'but I must now return to London and pursue the man who did this thing.'

Very shortly we were back in the station dogcart, rattling once more between bright meadows and pleasant gardens, but the day was shadowed by the grief of those two innocent women, drawn by chance into the strange drama that was developing in the capital.

7

THREE GOLDEN CIRCLES

The journey back to London was a long one, but both Holmes and I were silent for much of the distance. He filled his pipe as soon as our train left the station and leaned back against the antimacassar with closed eyes, evidently lost in consideration of the information gleaned in Gloucestershire. I was still oppressed by the reflection that a thrust of an assassin's knife-blade in London had brought grief and misery to a previously happy home on the other side of the country.

We were at Reading before my spirits had lifted sufficiently for me to purchase a newspaper. As we drew out I eyed its pages, which seemed to be filled with the forthcoming Jubilee celebration and the marvels of the Wild West Show at the American Exhibition.

A little while later Holmes knocked out his pipe and asked, 'Is there anything there of interest, Watson?'

I shook my head. 'Half of the royalty and nobility of the world have arrived or will soon arrive in London for the Jubilee,' I said, 'and many of them, together with most of London society, have been visiting Colonel Cody's show at Kensington. It seems strange to me that, as we prepare to celebrate the Crown and our Empire, the greatest attraction in England is a bunch of Americans!'

'Americans!' exclaimed Holmes. 'There you have it, Watson! Why so many Americans?'

'Whyever not?' I said, totally confused. 'It is after all a show devoted to matters American.'

'Not at Kensington, Watson, but in our enquiry,' he snapped. 'Wherever we look we find more Americans than Cody has brought with him. Why should that be?'

He flung out a long hand and with the forefinger of the other counted off his points as he continued.

'Firstly,' he said, 'Lestrade consults us about an attack by an apparent madman upon an American businessman who was in the company of that country's Minister.'

I nodded.

'Secondly, that seeming madman consults us, and appears to be not the Yorkshireman which he would have us believe, but an American or an Englishman who has spent much time in America. He complains that he is followed by two men, and their deaths have enabled us to determine that one of those men was an American and the other an Englishman who had passed most of his life in that country and had served the Confederacy both as a naval officer and as a spy.

'My own observations', he continued, 'led to Lestrade's information about the American Doctor. I say again, Watson, why so many Americans in this affair?'

'Well,' I hazarded, 'Lestrade says that Scotland Yard believes Tumbletye to be a Fenian from America, here to engineer some plot against Her Majesty's Jubilee. You and he were agreed about the considerable involvement of Americans with the Fenian Brotherhood.'

'True,' he agreed, 'but there is evidently far more to it than that. Littlechild is interested in Tumbletye because he believes him to be an American Fenian, so the Scotland Yarders follow the Doctor, but Tumbletye's interest seems to be in Byron and Scotland Yard has no apparent interest in him except Lestrade's concern about the incident with Candover. What is it that makes Tumbletye pursue Byron, Watson?'

I shook my head. 'I haven't the least notion,' I said.

'No more have I,' he admitted, 'and I have left out of the picture our two dead men. Their deaths convince me that I was right in my speculation that they meant no harm to Byron. They were set on by someone to observe and, perhaps, to protect him. But by whom, Watson? By whom?'

Again I was forced to confess to a total lack of ideas.

'An American and an Englishman who was to all intents an American,' mused Holmes. 'They were not Fenians, it seems, nor is Byron.'

'Why do you say so?' I asked.

'If Byron was a Fenian, Littlechild's men would follow him, not the dramatic Doctor. If they interposed themselves between Tumbletye and Byron it was most probably because they knew Tumbletye is a Fenian and had some reason for protecting Byron from him.'

'Do you believe that they were killed by Fenians?' I said.

'Who else, Watson?' he said. 'Who else? If, for whatever reason, Tumbletye has set his sights on Byron, then the presence of those two was an obstacle to his plan.'

'They were seamen,' I said. 'We know that the younger man frequented places of ill repute. Might they not have met their deaths in some whorehouse brawl on the Ratcliffe Highway?'

'How can you suggest it, Watson? You saw the bodies. Where were the marks of brawling? Where were the grazed knuckles, the bruises, the kick marks to the shin that are the hallmarks of such an encounter?'

'But they were knifed,' I protested.

'Where, then, were the cuts to the hands and arms, as they defended themselves? Why were their own weapons unused?' he demanded. He shook his head. 'No, Watson,' he said, 'they had no chance to defend themselves. They were taken by surprise and killed quickly and silently. A single, accurate blow to the head, followed by one thrust of a knife when they were helpless. Killings with expertise, Watson, and by the use of the same weapon that the Irish-American Invincibles employed in Phoenix Park.'

'But in Phoenix Park the victims were stabbed from the front, and Burke's throat was cut,' I protested.

'In Phoenix Park,' said Holmes, 'the attack was an ambush in broad daylight. Tremaille and his friend were most probably taken by surprise in some black waterside alley.'

'What steps will you take now?' I enquired.

'First,' he said, 'I must withdraw the Irregulars. I cannot leave Wiggins and his lads exposed to the kind of ruthlessness that we have seen. Then I must pursue the other clue that has emerged from our enquiries.'

'The other clue?' I repeated, somewhat surprised.

'The first clue, Watson, is the preponderance of American connections in this affair. The second is the Golden Circle.'

'The Golden Circle!' I said. 'Miss Tremaille mentioned a Golden Circle. But what is it, Holmes?'

'It is the third such that we have come across and it is the only apparent connection between John Byron and Ashley Tremaille.'

'I still do not understand,' I admitted.

'You have not asked what took us to Gloucestershire,' he said.

'The letter,' I said. 'Surely it was the letter in Tremaille's pocket?'

He laughed. 'The letter, Watson, would indeed have led us to Gloucestershire, and where else? To which doorstep in that wide county? I have, I admit, argued that it should be possible to infer the existence of the ocean from the known existence of a grain of sand, but even I would not have set out for Gloucestershire without some more detailed information. You have forgotten what I told you yesterday, that it was not merely the letter that drew me to Gloucestershire.'

'What then?' I asked.

'The Golden Circles,' he said.

'But it was Laura Tremaille who first mentioned a Golden Circle!'

'And that was not the first time that we had come across a Golden Circle,' he said. 'Do you not recall that I drew your attention to the ornate ring which Byron wears?'

'Yes,' I said, 'but I had not observed it as closely as you.'

'No,' he said, 'you had not. It was a heavy ring of first-class gold, but it carried no jewel nor seal, only an enamelled plaque bearing a design composed of Byron's three initials.'

'That is surely not significant,' I said.

'Not in itself, no, Watson, but the plaque bore also a thin circle of gold that cut across the edges of the monogram.'

'A decorative feature?' I suggested. 'The ring is a part of Byron's theatrical manner and mode of dress.'

'So it might be,' he agreed, 'but why take the trouble to have an ornate monogram constructed if it is to be partially obscured by the ring of gold? It would have been perfectly easy to reduce the size of the initials so that the design lay within the gold circlet, or to leave out the circle so that the entire monogram was displayed.'

I was silent and he continued. 'It might have been, as you suggest, merely a curious example of our client's melodramatic personality, but it caught my attention. It became more significant when I observed that the corpse of Ashley Tremaille wore a similar ring.'

'But that had no monogram,' I protested.

'No, indeed,' he said. 'It had an heraldic design, but it was again a heavy gold ring, mounted with an enamelled plaque, and the ornamentation on that plaque was partly within a thin circle of gold.'

'Coincidence,' I suggested.

He snorted. 'Watson!' he exclaimed. 'You should know better than to suggest coincidence to me. I have remarked often enough that it is merely the convenient excuse of the unthinking. That singular feature of the two rings led me to pay particular attention to the design on the dead man's ring.'

He drew a slip of paper from his coat pocket. 'Where have you seen that design?' he asked as he held out the paper to me.

It was the page from my pocket-book on which he had drawn at the mortuary. 'Why!' I exclaimed. 'That is the shield that was over the door in Gloucestershire!'

'Precisely, Watson,' he said. 'A call upon an acquaintance at the College of Heralds established that these are the ancient bearings of the Tremaille family and a glance at a directory of the landed gentry revealed the address of the family seat in Gloucestershire. It revealed also that there was an Ashley Tremaille in his forties, whose residence was in North Carolina. Even had I been a believer in coincidence, Watson, I could not have believed the two golden circlets, the coat of arms, the letter from Gloucestershire and an address in America to be coincidental.'

He sat back in triumph. 'Remarkable, Holmes!' I said. 'But what do you think is the significance of the golden circlets?'

'I suspect', he said 'that they serve the same purpose as the Welsh leek.'

'Holmes!' I complained. 'You are making fun of me!'

'Heaven forbid, my dear Watson! Do you not recall that Henry Tudor in preparation for his campaign against Richard III told his supporters to identify themselves to each other by the

54

background colours of the Welsh banner, green and white? And for that reason they pulled up leeks to show the white root and the green stem as the mark of their secret loyalty. The circleted rings are, I believe, the same. A less cumbersome object than a leek to keep about one's person and by which the members of a clandestine organisation might identify each other.'

'How will you pursue this clue?' I asked.

Holmes glanced out of the window, 'When we reach Paddington,' he said, 'I shall call upon a connection of mine who can assist me in respect of both the spies of the Confederacy and Americans presently in London.'

8

THE PRESIDENT'S MAN

At Paddington Station we separated, Holmes announcing that he was going to pursue the American connection in this affair and suggesting that I meet him at Craig's Antiquarian Bookshop in the Charing Cross Road two hours later.

Confused as I had become by the ever-increasing complexity of Holmes' enquiry, I had not forgotten that the bookshop had been the address at which Mrs Tremaille wrote to her son. Holmes, if he had formed any view as to the reason behind Tremaille's activities and his connection with the bookshop, had not informed me, so that I felt entitled to speculate as I wished about the real nature of the bookshop.

My first sight of the premises was disappointing. I think that I can claim a wide acquaintance with the antiquarian bookshops of London, and the majority are (and were at the period of which I write) distinguished largely by the quantities of dust which they accumulate, the disorder of the books upon their shelves and the gloom of their interiors, wherein lies much of their charm to the real bibliophile.

Mr Craig's premises were suspiciously clean and bright. Outside the paintwork was new, the windows recently cleaned and the chequered tiles in the doorway freshly scrubbed. Within were uniform ranks of white-painted shelves, set with books which had been carefully sorted into their proper categories.

At the rear of the shop a young man sat at a high desk. When I entered he came forward, enquiring if he could help me.

'No,' I said. 'I had not seen your shop before and merely stepped in to browse.'

He left me to it, and I paced the aisles of the shop, letting my gaze run over the tidy ranks of books like a reviewing General's. This was evidently not the kind of shop where one would find some sixteenth-century rarity, carelessly piled in a dusty jumble on a table labelled 'All at 2d'.

I had long grown bored with my inspection of the stock, and had slipped my watch out more than once to see if Holmes was due, when he appeared suddenly beside me.

'Have you added any volumes to your library, Watson?' he asked.

I shook my head. 'There is little here that interests me,' I said. 'I wonder that the trade sustains the premises. I have been here a full hour and a half and no other customer has been in.'

Holmes strode up to the clerk's desk. 'Tell me,' he said to the young man, 'do you keep American books? I was told so.'

'That is quite correct, sir,' said the assistant. 'We rather make a speciality of them. Was there something in particular that you required, sir?'

'Yes,' said Holmes. 'I wonder if you have a copy of Captain Ashley Tremaille's *Secrets of the Golden Circle*?'

The young man tilted his head, thoughtfully. 'Is that a work of fiction, sir?' he asked.

'No,' replied Holmes. 'It is a volume concerned with the Civil War in America.'

'Ah!' exclaimed the assistant, and slipping from his stool made his way to a particular case. I had already observed that its shelves were filled with military volumes. He scanned each shelf carefully, then returned shaking his head.

'I'm afraid that we do not have it at present, sir. Would you like us to make enquiries for a copy?'

'If Mr Craig is in, I shall be grateful if you will draw my enquiry to his attention,' said Holmes.

'I do not believe Mr Craig can do more than I have offered, sir, but if you think he can assist you I shall inform him,' said the assistant.

'Please take my card to Mr Craig,' said my friend and gave the young man a card.

The youth disappeared through a baize-curtained door at the rear of the shop, but was back in less than a minute.

'Mr Craig wonders if you could spare him a moment,' he said, and ushered us through the door.

The room into which he showed us was small and lined with shelves full of books. A single narrow window looked down upon a rear yard. From behind a desk there rose a large, fair man, darkly clad and bespectacled, but with a physique that suggested some more active occupation than that of a bookseller.

He dismissed his clerk and waved Holmes and me to two chairs in front of his desk. 'Now then, gentlemen,' he said, once we were seated, 'I am Pericles Craig. How can I help you?' I noticed that his accent, though unobtrusive, was American.

Holmes indicated his card where it lay upon the bookseller's desk. 'I am merely seeking a rare book,' he said.

'Mr Holmes,' said Craig, 'as England's most successful consulting detective – the man who advises Scotland Yard – you cannot be unaware that no such book exists. I ask again, in what way do you imagine I can help you?'

Holmes smiled thinly. 'You are remarkably well informed for a dealer in books, Mr Craig,' he said, 'but there is no question of my imagining that you can help me. I have been advised on good authority that you can, if you choose to, give me considerable help.'

'On what authority is that?' asked Craig.

Holmes drew a folded paper from his coat pocket and passed it across the desk. 'I would', he said, 'have presented this rather than my card and a request for a non-existent volume, but I did not wish your assistant to be aware of it.'

'Admirably discreet, Mr Holmes,' said the American and turned his attention to the paper.

When he looked up from his reading he was frowning. 'Even the person who signed this letter', he said, 'must know that I cannot reveal to you the secrets of my Government, Mr Holmes.'

Holmes clasped his long hands over the handle of his stick and leaned forward. 'Mr Craig,' he said, 'or Colonel Craig as I understand you to be, this is not a time when we should, in your American expression, "beat about the bush". The man who signed that note, despite his relationship to me, would never have revealed what he has unless he believed that the interests of the United States as well as those of the Empire were involved in my enquiry.'

'The interests of the United States are my affair, Mr Holmes,' said Craig, 'and I do not see how they have become yours.'

'I have been consulted', replied Holmes, 'by a minor writer of melodramas called John Byron. He believed himself, rightly as it proved, to be followed and had grown concerned. Now my client, though he describes himself as a Yorkshireman, I believe may well be an American.'

Craig started to speak, but my friend raised a hand to stop him. 'What is more,' Holmes continued, 'the men whom he had seen following him were an American and an Englishman who has lived for many years in your country. That is why I took the advice that has brought me to you.'

'Mr Byron', said Craig, slowly, 'is a gentleman who interests my Government for reasons which I cannot reveal to you. Since you have partly identified the men who follow him, you must be aware that they are not the only followers.'

'They no longer follow John Byron,' said my friend. 'Ashley Tremaille and his companion are both dead. I assume that your undisclosed interest in Mr Byron led you to assign them to protect him from the attentions of the American Fenian Tumbletye.'

Craig started back in his chair. 'Tremaille dead?' he said. 'I did not know. And you are aware of Tumbletye. How did they die, Mr Holmes? Was Tumbletye involved?'

'Both of them ended in the Thames after being scientifically stabbed with a surgical knife,' said Holmes. 'While I cannot positively assert that Tumbletye is responsible for their deaths, the method is that of the Invincibles and it seems that Tumbletye had a reason or reasons to put them out of his way. Now that your operations in this affair have led to the deaths of two of your men, perhaps you will see the wisdom of co-operating with my own enquiries, Colonel.'

Craig laid both hands flat upon his desk and looked long and steadily at Holmes. At length he said, 'There are two things here, Mr Holmes. One is the question of Byron and his commission to you; the other is the reason for Tumbletye's presence in London. I repeat – Byron is of interest to my Government for reasons which are of no consequence whatsoever to Britain.

My instructions are to see that no harm comes to him and that I was doing by assigning Tremaille and his companion.'

'It was their activities', interposed Holmes 'which so alarmed Byron that he sought my assistance.'

'Maybe so, Mr Holmes,' said Craig, 'but I had no alternative. My second point was Dr Tumbletye. You, of course, will be aware that, apart from his medicine show activities, he is an enthusiastic Fenian supporter. Your police believe him to be a conduit for both ideas and funds for the Invincibles.'

'And he is the business of our police while he is in this country, Colonel,' said Holmes.

'True, Mr Holmes, but it seems that he has developed an interest in Byron and that makes Tumbletye the business of the United States. Whatever Tumbletye's intentions in London they bode no good to Britain, on that we may both agree, but you must take my word for it that a conjunction of Tumbletye and Byron would be disastrous to both our countries.'

'Byron seems harmless enough,' said my friend

'Left to himself,' said Craig, 'Byron will pursue his scribbling and cause no problems to you, me or Scotland Yard but if that damned Doctor succeeds in entangling Byron in his plots I will not answer for the international consequences.'

'Then,' said Holmes, 'you had best help me insofar as you are able.'

'I will do what I can,' said the Colonel. 'In the first place I shall continue – as I must – to protect Byron.'

'I suggest that you do so in a less obvious fashion,' said Holmes.

'I had hoped that the presence of my men was so obvious that it would keep Tumbletye at bay. Evidently I was wrong. From now on my watch on Byron will be undetectable. In return I ask you to look to Tumbletye. For all that Scotland Yard knows of him he has defeated them for years. I am cheered to learn that you are on his trail, Mr Holmes.'

He pulled open a drawer of his desk and took out a slip of paper. After scribbling on it he passed it to Holmes.

'That', he said, 'is the name of a man who knows, I suspect, more about Tumbletye than Scotland Yard. He is an agency reporter from the States and has made the doings of

Dr Tumbletye something of a speciality. I suggest that you talk to him.'

'And where will I find him?' asked Holmes, rising.

The Colonel pulled out his watch and consulted it. 'Unless there is a major catastrophe in London, you should find him at the Green Dragon. By all means say that I sent you, but be discreet if you will, Mr Holmes.'

'The informant who referred me to you, Colonel, has good reason to trust me, as you know. You may do the same. Come, Watson, I believe you can lead me to the Green Dragon.'

9

DENIZENS OF THE GREEN DRAGON

I was, indeed, acquainted with the Green Dragon, a public house much favoured by writers, artists and reporters, though not through my own literary pretensions. In that summer I was completing my record of Holmes' enquiry in the Drebber affair and its future in print was still uncertain. I had come to know the hostelry through my friend Thurston who frequented it in order to hobnob with that extraordinary group of writers who worked for the *Sporting Times* – 'the Pink 'Un'. Playing billiards with Thurston at the Green Dragon I had made the acquaintance of Binstead who wrote as 'the Pitcher', Major Newnham-Davis, called for reasons I have never known 'the Dwarf of Blood', and others of that bright and amusing set who made the Pink 'Un so much more than a racing paper.

Thurston was not among the company when Holmes and I entered but Binstead and the Dwarf were sharing a table and hailed my appearance.

'Heavens!' cried Newnham-Davis. 'It's Watson come here with his pal the famous sleuth to lock us up. It's all up, Pitcher, we might as well make a clean breast of it!'

He held out his hands to Holmes as though for the handcuffs while Binstead joined his fingers over his ample stomach and said, 'I seem to recall that 'twas Thurston who first suggested sandpapering the billiard balls. I shall plead not guilty.'

'Gentlemen,' said Holmes, 'much as I believe you should both be locked up, if only to keep Watson from bankruptcy, I am here on another errand. Do either of you know an American called John Essex?'

They looked at each other with exaggerated solemnity. 'John Essex,' repeated Newnham-Davis. 'Now there's a villain worthy of you, Mr Holmes. A Yankee scoundrel who sits here by the hour, drinking good British ale and stealing from our newspapers the copy of hard-working British writers, which same he boils down to telegraphese and cables to New York in return for huge sums of money. You would do us all a favour by arranging his deportation.'

'I fear that I am merely seeking information,' said Holmes. 'I am interested in a certain Dr Tumbletye. Do any of you know him?'

'The American medicine man?' said the Dwarf. 'Can't say I know him, but I've seen him about town. Word has it that he's a thoroughly bad lot, mixed up with dynamiters and what have you. Johnny Essex has got a bit of a bee in his bonnet about him, says that Tumbletye is the greatest criminal in London.'

'A view which Scotland Yard seems to share,' said Holmes. 'Is Essex here?'

'Down the far end,' said Binstead. 'This time of day he's busy writing his stuff ready to use the cheap wires to New York at night. Tall fellow, red hair, brown tie, yellow shirt, green tweeds,' and he shuddered expressively.

Holmes thanked them and turned away. Newnham-Davis caught me by the sleeve. 'Merry Hampton for the Jubilee Derby,' he said in a low tone. 'Depend upon it.'

'But that's Abingdon's horse! The man's a scoundrel!' I exclaimed.

'Oh, drat the man!' said Newnham-Davis. 'Scoundrel or not, he's going to take the Derby first time out. Get on it, Watson!'

'What are you doing here?' I asked for I had thought him abroad with his regiment, but he had no chance to explain.

'Watson!' called Holmes, impatiently. 'Could you tear yourself away from the turf long enough to assist my enquiries?'

We made our way down the long bar until we spotted a man seated alone at a table littered with newspapers. He was dressed as Binstead had described and was a tall, lean man in his mid-thirties with pale sharply drawn features. As we stopped by his table he looked up from writing on a thick notepad.

'Dr Watson and Sherlock Holmes!' he exclaimed. 'What brings you here, Mr Holmes?'

'It was suggested that you might be able to assist me with information,' said Holmes.

'When I have finished digesting what your papers have to say about Cody's show at Earls Court I shall be happy to give you my attention, Mr Holmes, but I require a few more words yet before I have satisfied my masters. In the meantime let me get you something to drink.'

He raised his hand for a potboy and we gave our orders. In a few minutes he had completed his task and pushed his pad away from him.

'Now,' he said, 'I have fully informed my fellow citizens of the effect that Colonel Cody is having on England. Did you know that Queen Victoria has been to see the Wild West Show? She was so taken with it that she has commanded a special performance at Windsor on the eve of the Jubilee so that all her crowned and noble guests can see it. If you have not seen it, gentlemen, you should really make a point of it.'

'I fully intend to see what the Colonel has to offer,' said Holmes, 'but at present Watson and I are engaged in an urgent enquiry. Your colleagues at the *Sporting Times* suggested that you might be of assistance.'

'Ha!' snorted Essex. 'I have seen you before in their company, Doctor, but I doubt if they have ever referred to me as a colleague. They treat me as some kind of colonial pirate who amasses a fortune by stealing their stories whereas they are the guys who are paid a salary to hang about the theatres and the music halls and the race course and the restaurants. I merely sit here or in a poky little office and attempt to boil their vapourings down into good, robust American prose that won't cost my bosses too much on the wire – for which skilful operation I get paid a pittance per word. But I must say the idea of helping the great Sherlock Holmes appeals. Can I have the story exclusively, Mr Holmes?'

'I am not sure', said Holmes, 'that you can have the story at all, Mr Essex. I am instructed by a private client, whose affairs have become entangled in some fashion which I do not understand with the presence in London of an American called Tumbletye. At present I cannot reveal to you the identity of my client or the nature of my instructions and it may be that, even when the matter is unravelled, it is one that will have to remain confidential.'

'Mr Holmes,' said Essex, 'my bosses in the States would pay big money for an exclusive account of any of your cases, but Tumbletye's a real winner. He's been a story longer than I've been a reporter, ever since he was arrested in the Lincoln affair. You cannot ask for my help and not give me the story!'

'I am afraid that I must, for the reasons I have set out,' said Holmes. 'I have indications that Tumbletye's presence in London is regarded as a grave threat by Scotland Yard and Colonel Craig believes that the matter may involve the United States as well. He also believed that you might assist me.'

'Pericles Craig sent you!' exclaimed the reporter. 'And how exactly did you sniff out that gentleman? If you have found your way to Colonel Craig you really are good.'

Holmes nodded in acknowledgement of the compliment. 'In years of practice as a consulting detective one acquires contacts, Mr Essex, as does a journalist. It was one such that pointed me to Craig as a source of confidential information on Americans in Britain.'

'Not Scotland Yard, for certain,' said Essex. 'They have no idea of Craig's function.'

'No, it was not Scotland Yard, nor do I propose to make them aware of Colonel's Craig's activities. I accept his word that his operations are in no way the affair of our police. Equally I have, I think, succeeded in convincing him that there is a mutual interest in my present enquiry. Craig has lost two of his agents at the hands of Tumbletye or someone set on by Tumbletye.'

'You mean killed?' asked Essex.

'Since you read all our newspapers you will have seen that two unidentified sailors have been found dead in the Thames. I can tell you what the newspapers do not, that those men were Craig's agents and that Tumbletye was the cause of their deaths, whether he wielded the surgical knife or not.'

'You make this more difficult,' said Essex. 'Now it is not just a matter of an investigation of yours in London, but you say it touches the States, that two Americans have died in the affair, that Tumbletye had them killed. You are talking big headlines, Mr Holmes. Lots of words, unlimited cable facility and, at the end of it, lots of silver dollars for John P. Essex – if you will give me the story.'

'Mr Essex,' said Holmes, 'if I could pay for your information I should gladly do so, but my client is a man of no great means. The best I can say is this – that, if Colonel Craig sees no objection to the publication of a story at the end of my enquiries, and if it can be done without identifying my client, then there will be a story – if, indeed, you find that it merits big headlines and lots of words. I cannot, I think, go further than that.'

'And that's not very far,' complained the reporter. 'Pericles Craig believes that any activity of any American in England is a secret of the State Department or whoever really pays his wages if he thinks it is.'

He drummed his fingers on the table for a few moments staring with a sour expression at the litter of papers. Then he looked up. 'I've very little choice, have I? If I don't buy a ticket I can't win the sweepstake?'

'Eloquently put,' smiled Holmes, 'and very true.'

'What do you already know about Tumbletye?' demanded Essex.

Holmes leaned forward and steepled the fingers of his two hands. 'We know', he said, 'that Tumbletye is an American of Canadian birth. That he calls himself a doctor though he appears to hold no medical qualification. That he was arrested during the investigation into the assassination of President Lincoln because he was travelling under a false name and that name was the real name of a known Confederate agent.'

He paused and the American nodded without speaking. Holmes continued.

'His politics are avowedly Fenian. He speaks and publishes on their behalf in the United States. Scotland Yard believes him to be a contact between the Invincibles in Ireland and England and their backers in America. At present Scotland Yard believes that he is in London preparing some special outrage in connection with Her Majesty's Jubilee.'

'Which, if it occurred, would be the biggest story in England this year,' said Essex thoughtfully.

'Mr Essex!' I exclaimed. 'We are talking about a madman! Are you prepared to countenance more murders in England – an attack upon Her Majesty – a bomb outrage during the Jubilee celebrations – any of these or something unimaginably worse,

66

merely to guarantee a good story? Big headlines? Unlimited wordage and a profit to you?'

He looked at me without replying, then turned his gaze back to Holmes.

'What do you know of Tumbletye's private life?' he asked.

'Littlechild at the Yard believes that Tumbletye is sexually insane,' said Holmes. 'I have seen him often in the presence of large young men, but I cannot determine whether they are merely his minders or have a more intimate connection.'

'Oh, he's sexually insane all right,' said Essex. 'Rumour has it that he was once married to a woman who both betrayed and infected him. Since then he seems to have confined his affections to his own sex, but it goes further than that. He detests women – all women. Do you know that in his chambers he keeps cabinets of medical specimens? He has a display which he shows to the privileged that reminds one of the Medical Museum in Liverpool. Have you ever seen that?'

I nodded, for I had seen that wretched and unpleasant display.

'Tumbletye's collection puts it to shame, Doctor,' said Essex, 'and it is all specimens of the parts of women healthy or diseased. He shows it to visitors by way of convincing them that women are a snare, bent on leading young men into vice and disease.'

'You have seen this collection?' asked Holmes.

'Surely,' said Essex. 'I have had the privilege of dining with Tumbletye more than once and playing cards with him. Interesting evenings they were, but heaven help his guests if one mentions the fair sex. Then he mounts his hobby horse and preaches like a fanatic, opens his cabinets and shows his revolting exhibits and generally prays for the damnation of all womankind.'

'So you know where he lives?' said Holmes.

'I do,' replied Essex. 'Why do you ask?'

'I was considering that I might pay a call upon the good Doctor, perhaps in his absence.'

'Only with me along,' said Essex.

Holmes shook his head. 'I fear not,' he said. 'If I am to trifle with English law it will not be for the first time and, if it came to that, I would stand the penalty of the risk I took, but I really cannot involve you in such an affair, Mr Essex.'

'Then I don't think I can help you further,' said Essex.

Holmes stood up, silently, and turned away from the table. After a pace he turned back.

'Tell me, Mr Essex,' he asked, artlessly, 'do you know of a minor dramatist called John Byron?'

'Byron!' exclaimed Essex. 'What has he got to with all this?'

'Colonel Craig, who would not tell me what interest your Government has in a penniless playwright from Yorkshire, felt that the combination of Tumbletye and Byron was such as to threaten both our countries. Do you, perchance, know why?'

'Sit down, Mr Holmes,' said Essex, grimly. 'You should have told me from the first that this was about Byron.'

'Why?' asked my friend. 'Who is he?'

10

PRIVATE LIVES

'That doesn't matter for the moment,' said Essex.

'I disagree with you, Mr Essex,' said Holmes. 'I believe that Mr Byron may well be the key to this mystery. It was he whose attack on the American Candover alarmed Lestrade, despite its appearance of religious mania; it was he who consulted me about the men who followed him and upon investigation they turned out to be agents of your Government sent to protect him from Tumbletye. But what, Mr Essex, does Byron mean to Tumbletye? Something of sufficient gravity for him to have two men murdered, but how can an elderly, lame playwright from Yorkshire assist an Invincible plot to destroy Her Majesty's Jubilee celebration? I say again, who is John Byron?'

Essex stared at my friend. 'I do not know,' he said at length. 'No, Mr Holmes, that is the truth – I really do not know, and if I was certain I would not dare to tell you.'

'Then you have a suspicion?' asked Holmes.

'If I do,' said Essex, 'it is not one that I can reveal to you.'

'Then tell me one thing,' said Holmes. 'Is Byron an American?'

Essex shook his head. 'I cannot even tell you that.'

'He is,' declared Holmes. 'For if he were not, Colonel Craig would not behave as he does in respect of Byron.'

'Pericles Craig acts like a law unto himself when it suits him,' said Essex.

'Pericles Craig is well aware that he walks a tightrope in this country,' said Holmes. 'He is an illegitimate and unacknowledged representative of a foreign power, albeit an apparently friendly one. He may take liberties with our law, but not if he is likely to be caught. In this matter he has already left Scotland Yard pursuing the killer or killers of his two agents. He must know that the risk to him and his duties is increasing by the minute. Byron must be both an American citizen and of great importance to the United States to impel Craig to take such a risk.'

'Mr Holmes,' said Essex, 'I am not being wilfully unhelpful but I assure you that firstly, I know nothing for certain of the reasons for Craig's interest in Byron; and secondly, if I even hinted to you what I suspect about Byron, Pericles Craig would have me whipped into a Federal prison for the rest of my life.'

Holmes looked at the reporter silently for some time. Then, 'Very well,' he said, 'if you cannot tell me about Byron, tell me about Tumbletye. You have your sources in this city and you know the man well enough to play at cards with him. Are the Scotland Yarders right in their suspicions of him?'

'Yes,' said Essex without hesitation. 'At home Tumbletye is a noisy supporter of the Fenian Brotherhood; here he is certainly involved in their plots. He believes that all freedom-loving Americans embrace the cause of the Irish and speaks fairly freely in American company. He is certainly party to a Fenian plot against Her Majesty.'

'And the nature of that plot?' asked Holmes.

'If I knew that, I should have informed Scotland Yard. I only know that Tumbletye boasts of a blow to be struck at the Jubilee that will shame England and America.'

'Why should he strike at America? There are many Irish there and many Fenian sympathisers.'

'He declares himself to be the victim of persecution in the States, ever since his arrest in the Lincoln plot.'

'And you do not know when he will strike?'

'I imagine that with his taste for the melodramatic he will choose the Jubilee ceremonies as his stage, to create the maximum impression.'

Holmes nodded. 'That seems probable and means we have very little time. Tell me, if you can, what is the connection between Tumbletye and Byron?'

Essex shook his head. 'Even if I am right in my suspicions of Byron, I know of no direct connection between them.'

'Is it perhaps', said Holmes, 'because they were both once members of the Knights of the Golden Circle?'

Essex whistled softly. 'You don't say so!' he exclaimed. 'Now that I did not know, Mr Holmes. Are you sure?'

'I am sure that Byron was,' said my friend. 'Perhaps you can tell me if Tumbletye was.'

Essex nodded. 'He wears a ring. He has shown it to me. He says it is the proof of his loyalty to the Confederacy in the war. Certainly I have heard that while he hung about Washington, pretending to be some kind of medical attaché, on Maclellan's staff, he was spying for the South.'

'What more do you know of the Golden Circle?' asked Holmes.

'It was a body of men who seem to have appointed themselves as spies and secret agents for the Confederate States.'

'Tell me, if you know,' said Holmes, 'was Sempford Candover a member of the Golden Circle?'

'Sempford Candover!' exclaimed Essex. 'Why, he well might have been, Mr Holmes. A lot of guys who were in the war say that Candover did something secret then, and some say he did it for both sides. But what's your interest in Candover?'

'Like you, Mr Essex, I am fascinated by newspapers. Surely it has not escaped you that Mr Byron assaulted Candover in the lobby of a theatre recently?'

'Oh, sure,' said Essex, 'but I couldn't figure out why. Do you know, Mr Holmes?'

Holmes shook his head. 'Lestrade at the Yard was present and he thinks it was religious mania but I am far from agreeing with him. In my experience religious mania has a logic of its own. It fastens on certain images or ideas and repeats them endlessly. But if the newspapers reported accurately what Byron screamed at Candover then it was a hodge-podge of religious names from the Bible and from the classics. Much as a poor playwright might construct for the character of a religious lunatic.'

'And Byron writes plays,' said Essex.

'Precisely,' acknowledged Holmes. 'It is far from impossible that Byron, for reasons I have yet to fathom, wished to be perceived as a religious maniac.'

'It might be a covert method of passing a message,' I suggested.

71

'A remarkably complex and unlikely one,' said Holmes. 'Why should not Byron communicate with Candover? Whatever Colonel Craig and our friend here know or suspect about Byron, so far as anyone else is concerned he is a matter of no interest. Candover was merely an unknown American in London for the Jubilee. Byron might have written to Candover at his hotel in complete confidence. We have, after all, Watson, ten posts daily here in London. No, he was not delivering a message. It is my belief that he was genuinely surprised and angered by the sight of Candover and sprang to the attack heedlessly, but the motive for that attack and the purpose of the gibberish that he shouted elude me.'

'The meaning?' I queried. 'I thought that you deemed it senseless.'

'I said the purpose, Watson – not the meaning. It is its very lack of any meaning that makes its purpose so obscure,' snapped Holmes.

He turned back to Essex. 'And you know nothing of Candover, beyond rumours of a dubious past in your Civil War?'

'He has business interests of some kind in the Western States, in Canada and here in England. That is what brings him to London. He seems to have friends in high places if he goes to the theatre with our Minister.'

Holmes nodded. 'Mr Essex,' he said, 'there are two favours which you might do me if you would. Firstly I should be happy to pay for any further information you can obtain about Candover – his past, his present reasons for being in London, any possible connection with Byron or Tumbletye or both.'

'Leave Byron out of your question and I'll be happy to oblige,' said Essex.

'Very well,' conceded Holmes, 'Let us leave Byron out. My second request is a much simpler one. Do you have Tumbletye's address?'

'Surely,' said the reporter, and pulled out his pocket-book. He thumbed through it and then copied an address on to a leaf of his notebook and handed it to Holmes. 'You are going to call on him?' he asked.

'I may do so,' said Holmes, slipping the note into his own pocket-book.

'Then be careful,' said Essex. 'He surrounds himself with large young men. They're not just the objects of his unnatural instincts. They're a kind of bodyguard. Tumbletye is a whole-hearted coward and they are around him to see that nobody gives him any trouble.'

'I have seen some of his young minders,' said Holmes. 'Hulking louts out of Stepney and Whitechapel, but they will not bother Watson and me. Neither of us is less than useful with a small pistol and I hold a black belt in the Japanese discipline of Baritsu, if you know of it.'

'I do,' said Essex, 'and I'm impressed. But remember, Tumbletye's boys won't fight fair.'

'Nor shall I,' smiled Holmes. 'In any case, I was not proposing to call while the Doctor is at home.'

Essex's eyes widened. 'You're going to burglarise his joint?' he exclaimed.

'I think the English vernacular is "to crack his crib",' smiled Holmes, 'but I had something along those lines in mind.'

'Take me along,' said Essex.

'Mr Essex,' said Holmes, 'you are evidently young and fitter than the life of a metropolitan journalist would suggest, but I really cannot involve you in this matter.'

'You could use my help,' urged the reporter.

'And you could use the story,' said Holmes. 'Nevertheless, I cannot permit an American citizen to join me in a serious breach of English criminal law. Think how I should feel if matters ended with you in one of our prisons!'

'I'll take that chance,' said Essex, eagerly. 'Listen, you said you'd give me the story if you could – think how much more valuable it will be if I can say that I had participated.'

'Very valuable, no doubt,' agreed Holmes, 'but how long do you think Scotland Yard would ignore headlines in the American press stating that Britain's only consulting detective was a burglar? I am not universally admired at the Yard and I think the answer to my question would be minutes rather than hours. No, Mr Essex, I am grateful for your offer, but I shall do my own law-breaking. Watson will, if he chooses, accompany me as he has done before, driven, I believe, by the same boredom and curiosity that lead him to fritter his income on unlikely horses.

We must bid you good day, Mr Essex. You know where to find me if you have information about Candover or Tumbletye.'

The reporter nodded. 'I do, Mr Holmes, but I say again – be careful with Tumbletye's boys.'

As we returned to Baker Street by cab I asked Holmes what he made of the American's information.

'I am not sure,' he said, thoughtfully. 'We have picked up more pieces of the puzzle, but what is the puzzle about? Looked at from one direction it might seem that some purely American drama is taking place in London, one which seems to have a root or roots in their Civil War. That would explain Candover, Byron, Tumbletye, Tremaille, Craig and the Golden Circle. But if that were the case, where does Tumbletye's Fenian connection fit into the picture? No, Watson, I cannot place those pieces I possess in their proper order. I must give a great deal more thought to it.'

Which is exactly what he did. Hardly were we back in our rooms when he flung himself at length upon the couch, lit his pipe and closed his eyes. That was how I left him, hours later when I retired to bed.

11

BYRON RETURNS

Holmes had not, it seemed, moved from the couch when I came down in the morning. The room was grey with the stale smoke of his shag. He ignored my greeting until I opened the windows.

'Ah, Watson,' he said. 'As determined upon fresh air as ever.'

'Really, Holmes,' I expostulated, 'I cannot imagine why you believe you can think better when your brain is filled with tobacco-smoke.'

He swung his long legs to the floor and smiled. 'There is something in tobacco which alerts the cells of the brain, Watson, that fires the thinking process. One day it will be recognised as an enormous boon to mankind. Statues of Walter Raleigh will be in every public square.'

As a doctor I was inclined to believe that the future would see the use of tobacco made illegal, along with alcohol, opium, cocaine and all those other useless drugs whose sole purpose seems to be the provision of transitory pleasure at the cost of health, but I forbore to dispute the point.

'Shall I ring for breakfast?' I asked.

'By all means,' he said, 'and in the meantime I shall shave.'

He returned to the sitting-room just as Mrs Hudson began to lay breakfast, and attacked his food with a will. I was cheered, for I knew this to be a sign that his reflections had dictated some clear course of action and he no longer felt the frustration which, at the worst, drove him to the cocaine bottle.

We had eaten and Holmes sat, still in his dressing-gown, leafing through the last of the morning's papers when I referred to our conversation in the cab.

'Have you reached any conclusions in the Byron affair?' I enquired.

'As to what must be done, yes,' he replied, 'but I am no nearer unravelling the matter. It is really a satisfyingly singular puzzle and certainly more than a mere three-pipe problem.'

'And what will you do?' I asked.

'The business of analysis, Watson, almost invariably begins with a few random facts, the association between which the analyst may not know. It is then his task to seek further data – more pieces of the puzzle, as it were – and when he has them, to turn them about and about in his mind until a pattern becomes evident.'

'What sort of pattern?' I asked.

'Watson, Watson,' he chided, 'how often have you heard me remark that to commence an analysis with a preconceived notion as to the pattern it will reveal is a guarantee that you will see that pattern – whether it is there or not. It is the besetting sin of the Scotland Yarders that, so far from investigating an event thoroughly to see if its patterns point to any particular individual, they clap the darbies upon some unlucky wretch and then look at the event with a view to establishing their suspect's guilt.'

He poured himself a cup of tea and sipped it. 'It is very much like those puzzle pictures that are cut into irregularly shaped pieces. In this affair,' he continued, 'the pieces with which we began were Lestrade's religious maniac and Byron's request for help. Soon we discovered Tremaille and Tumbletye and all of this, though unclear, made a kind of sense.'

'I don't believe I understand you,' I said.

'Imagine, if you will, that we began work upon the left-hand side of the picture. That side, through Candover, Byron, Tremaille, Tumbletye and Craig, reveals a strong American pattern. However, the pieces of the right-hand side, as it were, come from Lestrade with his Fenian connection, which Essex confirms. They would seem, almost, to be part of a different picture, were it not for the presence of Tumbletye. We are left, Watson, without a large central area of our picture nor do we have any pieces to fill it.'

'Then what will you do?' I asked again. 'Colonel Craig appears to hold some of those pieces but will not reveal them. Essex believes he knows what some of them are, but is afraid of Craig. Where will you find more data?'

'I shall examine carefully those details which we do possess,' he said. 'By noting a line here, an area of colour there, on both sides of the gap it should, eventually, become possible to deduce the nature of the missing pattern.'

'By what means?' I said.

'Firstly by talking to the singular Mr Byron once more and secondly by examining Tumbletye in a little more detail.'

As events turned out, it required no effort to carry out the first part of my friend's plan, for we had barely finished luncheon when Mrs Hudson announced the arrival of our mysterious client.

When Byron joined us Holmes offered him the basket chair and plied him with a cigar and a brandy and soda. Despite the warmth of the afternoon our client still wore his cloak, but his yellowed features seemed paler than before and shadows hung under both eyes.

When our guest had taken a drink Holmes smiled at him. 'I am pleased to see you, Mr Byron,' he said, 'for I have good news.'

'Good news?' said Byron. 'What good news, Mr Holmes?'

'It has surely not escaped your notice that the two followers who dogged your footsteps have disappeared,' said Holmes.

'Oh, indeed,' said Byron. 'They have been absent for a couple of days, but is that permanent? Have they really given up?'

'I can assure you,' said Holmes, 'that those two will not cause you any further disquiet.'

'Then I can only say that I am deeply grateful to you, Mr Holmes. Please let me have a note of your fees and whatever sum you charge I shall strive to pay.'

'My charges,' said Holmes, 'only vary when I choose to remit them completely – as I do in your case, Mr Byron.'

The writer looked startled, rather than pleased.

'No, no, Mr Holmes. You have relieved me of a great burden, Mr Holmes, and must be properly rewarded.'

Holmes smiled. 'I pursue my singular avocation,' he said, 'for the cerebral stimulation which it provides. You have brought me a very pretty problem, several aspects of which remain unrevealed to me. It would be a shame to charge you for the pleasure you have given me. However, you might amply repay my small services by answering some questions which have arisen in the course of my enquiries if you will.'

A flicker of unease passed across Byron's features. 'Of course I will – if I can,' he replied.

'You might begin,' said Holmes, 'by explaining what drove you to attack Candover at the theatre.'

'I do not know what you mean,' said Byron. 'I know – '

Holmes lifted a commanding hand to cut him short. 'Pray do not trifle with me, Mr Byron,' he said sternly. 'Shortly before you enlisted my aid, you were seen to launch an attack upon Candover when he accompanied the American Minister to a theatre.'

'I had hoped,' said Byron, 'that you were unaware of that unfortunate incident.'

'It is my business to be aware of events that concern my clients,' said Holmes.

'It was a – a sudden rage – a moment of folly. The sudden sight of that man overwhelmed my senses – I – I . . . ' He stammered to a halt.

'He is evidently a man who has wronged you, Mr Byron,' said Holmes.

'Oh, aye!' exclaimed the playwright. 'Wronged me he has – made me his dupe, destroyed my life, but still I have fared better at his hands than some. For what little my life is worth, at least I have it.'

'He has killed friends of yours?' asked Holmes quietly.

Byron shook his head slowly. 'He is too sly to kill with his own hands, but he slew them as surely as if he had poisoned them.' He looked my friend in the eye and his face was paler yet. 'This is a matter which you do not want to know, Mr Holmes. It was all a long time ago, in another country.'

He fell silent, gazing at the floor.

'Then perhaps you will tell me one more thing,' said Holmes. 'What is your real name?'

Byron lifted his head and stared at Holmes. 'Why should you think I have any other name?' he demanded.

'Because,' said my friend, 'I have consulted the Green Books of the East India Company. There has never been a Collector or Assistant Collector of your name. I do not doubt that you have

78

been in India maybe as a servant of John Company but not under the name you bear now.'

Byron laughed a thin ugly laugh. I heard an undertone of hysteria in it and remembered the attack upon Candover.

'I have been in many countries, Mr Holmes, and under many names, but none of this concerns you. Here and now I am John Byron, playwright.' He heaved himself out of the basket chair. 'You have completed your commission for me, Mr Holmes. I have thanked you and I stand ready to pay you. I owe you no explanations.'

He was at the door when Holmes spoke softly. 'And Dr Tumbletye?' he asked. 'Do you not wish me to deal with him?'

Byron whirled so fast he almost lost his balance stumbling against the door jamb.

'Tumbletye!' he hissed. 'What of Tumbletye?'

'Whoever were the men whom you feared, Mr Byron, they are gone, but your steps were also followed by Dr Tumbletye – and still are.'

Byron's face had collapsed into a mask of pallor and shadow. His black eyes were wide with fear.

'Tumbletye follows me?' he said in a hollow tone, and Holmes nodded.

'Can you not stop him?' asked Byron.

'I do believe so,' said Holmes, placidly, 'if you so instruct me.'

'Instruct you,' echoed Byron. 'I cannot bear the thought of being followed by that filthy lunatic. I instruct you, Mr Holmes – nay, I plead with you. Stop Tumbletye at all costs!'

With no other word he flung open the door and reeled away down the stairs.

12

A LITTLE EXERCISE IN BLOOMSBURY

As our client's footsteps faded down the stairway I sprang to my feet, intending to follow, but Holmes restrained me with an outflung arm.

'But Holmes!' I exclaimed. 'The man is evidently sick and you have thoroughly frightened him. Who knows what he may do!'

'He was thoroughly frightened when he first consulted me,' said Holmes. 'He was frightened of Craig's men, perhaps because he did not know who sent them or perhaps because he did. He was shocked by Candover's appearance in London. For whatever reason he dared not go to the police. He consulted me and he now believes that I removed Craig's men. Fearful as he is of Tumbletye he heard my promise to remove the threat and he will rely on that.'

'I still fear that he may harm himself,' I said. 'He is evidently under alarming strain.'

'He is, I suspect,' said Holmes, 'a man who has lived under great strain for a very long time. If he were suicidal he would not be alive now.'

'You seem to take this all very calmly,' I protested. 'Do you believe that you can stop Tumbletye?'

'Certainly,' he replied, 'once I know why he hounds Byron, and I expect to have some indications of his reasons within days. It will depend upon the weather.'

I had come to recognise that apparently illogical remarks by my friend were often nothing more than bait to lure me into asking a question. I did not always oblige and was, thereby, forced to remain in ignorance of the connection between Tumbletye and the weather.

It was one of the extraordinary features of Holmes' personality that he would drive himself for days without rest or food when in pursuit of an urgent investigation and he would pass sleepless nights in analysis of cases that had come to a standstill, but when a course of action had been identified, if it could not be pursued immediately he would turn to some other subject as though he had nothing else to concern him.

In the days that followed he spent much of his time at his chemical bench, making our sitting-room obnoxious with the vapours he created and earning black looks from Mrs Hudson whenever she entered.

There came an evening when I could stand the poisoned atmosphere no longer. I flung open the window and announced that I proposed to go out for some fresh air.

Holmes looked up from his test tubes and gazed out of the window with an abstracted air. Then, 'Excellent!' he declared. 'You are exactly right – fresh air is necessary. If you will bear with me for a moment, I shall be happy to accompany you.'

With hindsight I should have considered that my friend, though physically strong and athletically skilled, was not a man who took exercise for its own sake but I was so pleased to have distracted him from his experiments that I overlooked the unusual nature of his response.

We set out a few minutes later. To my amazement, Holmes had armed himself with a stick which I had not seen before and, though the spring evening was warm and overcast, he wore a long coat. I had intended merely to take a turn in the park, but to my further astonishment Holmes turned in the opposite direction and made for the cab rank by Tussaud's where he jumped into a cab and asked the cabbie to take us to Bloomsbury.

'Bloomsbury, Holmes?' I queried.

'Yes, Watson, Bloomsbury,' he replied. 'I told you that my actions were dependent on the weather and tonight's weather will suit my purposes entirely.'

It was then that I began to suspect that my innocent evening's recreation had been transformed into a criminal enterprise.

In Bloomsbury Holmes paid off our cab at an anonymous crossroads and led me down a side street, stopping before a three-storeyed house whose front ground-floor window showed a light.

'There', he said pointing with his stick, 'is the home in London of Dr Tumbletye.'

'You propose to visit him?' I asked.

'He is not, I hope, at home,' said Holmes. 'I took the precaution of sending Byron a complimentary ticket for a theatre. If Byron goes to the play it will be most likely that Tumbletye will follow him. Besides,' he continued, 'while the lower storey is lighted where his landlady sits in her room, there is no light above.'

'You intend to burgle his rooms,' I stated.

'Exactly,' said Holmes. 'You are, of course, entirely at liberty to withdraw at this point.'

Holmes' occasional ventures into criminality always disturbed me but I had no intention of permitting him to run the risk alone.

'Of course I shall come with you,' I said, 'but how are we to enter if his landlady is in residence?'

'Good fellow,' said Holmes. 'I knew I could rely on you. We shall enter silently and from the rear.'

He led me along a path beside the house where an unlocked gate in a low wall gave us access to the back garden of Tumbletye's home. Holmes scanned the back of the house.

'We are in luck,' he said. 'There is no light at the back and the Doctor's landlady has left a stair window slightly open on this warm evening.'

He unscrewed the handle of his stick and, reaching into his coat pocket, drew out a device with which he replaced it. Now his stick ended in two strong wide metal hooks. He made a further adjustment and began to extend the stick in telescopic sections. As each section emerged he pulled from it a lever-like device which then protruded at right angles from the shaft. Soon he had a metal tube some ten feet long, with short projections at intervals of about one foot.

'Jacob's Ladder,' he announced softly, and lifted the device so that its two hooks settled on the sill of the open window. After tugging at it to ensure that it was firmly in place, he swarmed up its shaft and invited me to follow. I was uncertain of the strength of the device, but found it remarkably stable. Soon both of us stood on the landing inside the window and Holmes' remarkable ladder had become a walking stick once more.

'A match if you please, Watson!' hissed Holmes and I passed him a box. He produced a small dark lantern from his coat pocket and lit it, narrowing its beam to the slenderest thread.

'Now,' he said, 'it is most likely that Tumbletye's sitting-room and study are on this level. Let us see.'

He opened the nearest door and I followed him into a large, well-furnished sitting-room. It was heavy with ornate drapes and reeked of some strange scent that reminded me of my days in India. Holmes closed the lantern's shutter, for the curtains were open and, despite the overcast sky, there was sufficient light to pick our way across to a door opposite us.

It was evidently Tumbletye's study, a square room lined with bookcases though one wall was taken up by two wide cupboards. Holmes tried their handles and found them locked.

'Take the lantern, Watson,' he commanded, 'and throw a narrow beam on the lock.'

I did as he requested while he extracted from his pocket a bunch of slender instruments which I had seen him apply before, and in seconds he had the door open.

He took the lantern from me and, widening its beam, shone it into the cupboard. From floor to ceiling the shelves were filled with large medical specimen jars. As a doctor I have witnessed a good many unpleasant sights, but I cannot forget the revulsion that I felt when I realised that each jar contained preserved portions of human flesh, all of them female and taken from the more intimate parts of the body. Each bore some deformity, injury or mark of disease.

Holmes shook his head in wonder. 'This is evidently the "museum" of which Essex spoke,' he said. 'Littlechild appears to be right in his view of the darkness of Tumbletye's mind.'

He turned to the second cupboard and in seconds revealed a similar display inside it. Closing both sets of doors and relocking them he crossed the room to a writing desk.

'Kindly stand between the desk and the window,' he requested, 'so that I may broaden the lantern's beam.'

'Should I not close the curtains?' I asked.

'No,' he said. 'Tumbletye has left them open and the window is visible from the street. If he were to return before we leave, he might well realise that an intruder had closed them. Equally I do not wish the lantern's light to be visible from the street.'

I stood where he directed and he placed the lantern on a cabinet beside the desk. There were no papers on the desk's top, only a blotter, and Holmes sorted rapidly through each of the desk's drawers in turn. He seemed to have found nothing of consequence when he paused suddenly and raised a hand.

'Listen!' he hissed. 'A four-wheeler is drawing up in the street.'

I stepped across to the window and looked down. Sure enough, a four-wheeler with blinds drawn was standing a few yards away from the front of the house.

Behind me Holmes said, 'You have allowed them to see the lantern's light, Watson. We must withdraw.'

Quickly he closed the drawers of the desk and snatched the lantern, slamming its shutter closed. I followed him through to the landing where he rapidly extended his ladder and set it in place, motioning me to climb first.

When we had reached the ground I waited for his instructions. First he took my pistol from his pocket and passed it to me.

'I took the liberty of bringing your Adams,' he said 'in case we ran into difficulty.'

'But Holmes!' I protested. 'We cannot shoot at police officers or innocent civilians!'

'The four-wheeler contains neither,' he said. 'It is Tumbletye's, and he prefers it to a hansom because he can carry more than one of his young men along with him.'

'Then we are in for a scrap,' I said.

'Indeed,' he said, 'and a dangerous one. Remember that Tumbletye's men favour the knife.'

We slipped out of the garden's side gate and made our way stealthily towards the street. When we reached it Holmes peered ahead.

'There is no one in sight,' he said, 'though the carriage still stands with the blinds down. They may be inside.'

As he spoke a footfall sounded on the dark path behind us. We both turned, Holmes whipping open the slide of his little lantern and lifting it.

It shone full on the face of a large young man who recoiled from the light. In an instant Holmes lunged at him with his stick, whirling it in the air like a rapier.

'Into the street, Watson!' he cried. 'Let us fight in the open!'

I plunged into the street and Holmes followed, still keeping the youth at bay. As we emerged from the path another young man dropped from the door of the carriage and ran towards us. I saw the lamplight flash on a long-bladed knife and pointed my pistol.

'Stop where you are!' I commanded. 'I shall not hesitate to shoot!'

He stopped short and I moved cautiously towards him, still keeping my pistol pointed at his midriff. He was about twenty years old, tall and muscular, one of those typical products of Stepney and Whitechapel who choose not to work but to deploy their muscles more profitably. He wore the bell-bottomed velveteens and embroidered waistcoat of his type, with a wide belt bearing his name worked in brass wire.

Behind me I could hear sounds of battle where Holmes was dealing with the other youth, but anxious as I was to go to his assistance I dared not take my eyes off my prisoner.

'Drop your knife!' I commanded, and he did so. 'Now, kick it towards me!'

He did so, and I picked it up, keeping him at gunpoint.

'Take off your belt!' I ordered him.

'Have an 'eart, guvnor,' he whined. 'The Doctor said as you was burgling his gaff.'

'Even if we had been,' I said, 'that is scarcely an excuse for coming at us with a knife. Now, take off your belt and kick it towards me!'

Reluctantly he did as ordered. Once the belt was off he required both hands to prevent his trousers from falling. I stepped behind him, thrust the muzzle of my Adams into the small of his back and with my free hand, threaded his belt between his elbows and buckled it tightly behind. Now he was secured. He could only support his trousers at the back and if he tried to loosen the belt they would fall.

I turned from my prisoner to see Holmes and his assailant wrestling vigorously. A knife, the twin of that carried by my

85

attacker, lay near to them and I picked it up. It was the long-bladed knife used by police surgeons to open cadavers, an exceedingly ugly and unusual weapon for an East End lout.

I stepped around Holmes and his opponent, trying to find an advantage where I could bring my pistol to bear, but the battle was fast-moving.

Holmes seemed to be giving at least as good as he got and eventually broke free. The ruffian lunged at him, a mistake which I had seen others make with Holmes. My friend stepped adroitly to one side, there was a blur of his arms in the air and the youth flew upwards, turning in the air to fall heavily on his back with a shriek of pain and surprise. In a flash Holmes was on him like a rat at a terrier, seizing the winded lout's throat and kneeling across his midriff. It was then that I heard the shriek of a police whistle and the sound of pounding feet. At the same time Tumbletye's four-wheeler rattled away into the darkness.

'I think', said Holmes, 'that you may put away the pistol now, Watson.'

13

THE REWARDS OF CRIME

A police Sergeant and a constable ran up to us, quickly followed by a second constable.

'What's going on?' demanded the Sergeant then recognised my friend. 'Why, Mr Holmes!' he exclaimed. 'Are you having a spot of bother, sir?'

'I believe, Sergeant,' said Holmes, 'that Dr Watson and I have accidentally disturbed these ruffians about to break into a dwelling-house. My friend and I had turned aside from our stroll to relieve ourselves in the alleyway along there and upon emerging were set upon by these two.'

'You seem to have given as good as you got, or more so,' commented the Sergeant.

'I have reached a certain degree of skill in the Japanese art of Baritsu,' said Holmes, 'which occasionally surprises my opponents.'

The constables had already taken custody of Tumbletye's men and the Sergeant looked them over with a professional eye.

'Not the sort as has any reason to be in these parts,' he said, 'unless it's a felonious one. We shall take care of them, Mr Holmes.'

'Thank you, Sergeant,' replied Holmes. 'They seem to be well equipped for burglary. Look there!' He pointed to the gutter where his remarkable stick and the little dark lantern lay.

The Sergeant whistled softly as he recovered the stick and lamp. 'A Jacob's Ladder!' he exclaimed. 'I haven't come across one for a while. Looks like you've caught a real pair of cracksmen here, Mr Holmes.'

'They may be more than cracksmen, Sergeant,' said Holmes. 'If you have a word with Inspector Lestrade at the Yard you will find he is interested in two unsolved murders which were committed with a long, thin-bladed weapon of some kind.

Something like these, perhaps,' and he took the two knives from my hand and held them under the Sergeant's lamp.

'Nasty-looking things, sir,' remarked the Sergeant. 'I can't say as I've ever seen anything quite like them before.'

'I suspect that you will have seen one before,' said Holmes. 'They are surgeon's post-mortem knives.'

'We're most grateful to you, Mr Holmes,' said the officer. 'Perhaps you will be kind enough to look in at your convenience and make a statement regarding the attack on yourself and Dr Watson by this pair?'

'I should not think so,' replied Holmes. 'Neither the Doctor nor I have sustained any harm and I think Inspector Lestrade's interest in these two may be much more important, Sergeant. Thank you for your timely assistance and goodnight.'

The Sergeant knuckled his helmet and we strolled away.

'Holmes!' I exclaimed when we were out of earshot of the officers. 'What will happen when those ruffians tell the police the truth?'

Holmes laughed. 'That is the least likely outcome of the matter,' he said. 'To explain their presence in this vicinity they will have to admit that they were riding as minders in Tumbletye's carriage, and I am certain that he will not permit his minions to draw police attention to his activities.'

'And what of the ladder and the lantern?' I asked.

'Those, I admit, are a nuisance,' he said. 'The lantern I can readily replace, but the Jacob's Ladder was constructed for me by old Mosely in Wednesbury. When I am next in the Black Country I must call upon him. It is not the sort of thing one can safely order by post.'

'I was thinking more of their supposed possession by Tumbletye's men,' I said.

'They are not, in themselves, proof of burglary, though they might support a charge of intent, and I should be very surprised if those young men had never harboured a felonious intent related to the property of others.'

'But the knives!' I protested. 'You have as good as accused them of murder!'

'And do you not think, Watson, that their connection with the American Doctor and their possession of two such curious weapons strongly suggests that they may, indeed, be the guilty parties? I doubt that Lestrade will succeed in constructing a hanging case against them but if he were to it would not disturb my conscience. No, Watson, they are likely to spend a few uncomfortable days in the cells at Cannon Row while Lestrade and the Sergeant investigate their possible misdeeds and if they are not charged with intent to break and enter or murder they will, at the least, have had a little time to consider the way in which they conduct themselves and the company they keep.'

He strolled along casually, hands held behind his back, but I could not help reflecting that we had come very close to death or injury at the hands of Tumbletye's villains or at the best, arrest for burglary – and we had achieved nothing.

We had returned to our lodgings and were supping on a bottle of claret and one of Mrs Hudson's admirable pies when Holmes took up the point.

'You seem disgruntled, Watson,' he remarked.

'Disgruntled', I said, 'is not the half of it! You know that I do not hesitate to accompany you, even when you choose to break the law, but tonight we have come unpleasantly close to being knifed by a pair of guttersnipes or to being carted off by the police as common burglars – all to no purpose whatsoever!'

He chuckled. 'Watson, Watson,' he said, 'if you think I am cavalier with your loyalty, I apologise wholeheartedly. I am as nothing without my good right arm.'

The apology and compliment mollified me somewhat, but there remained the fact that our adventure in Bloomsbury had gained us nothing.

'It still seems to me to have been a foolhardy risk for no benefit,' I protested.

'Not so, Watson, not so,' he said and reached into his coat pocket.

He drew out a small paper packet and unfolded it before offering it across the table.

It was a half-Imperial sheet of pink blotting-paper. It had been creased once, firmly, across the middle and later folded down into smaller areas.

'Surely,' said Holmes, raising an eyebrow, 'you did not believe that I would put you in the shadow of Pentonville and come away empty-handed?'

I examined the paper. It had been used to blot something written in green ink but I was able to make little sense of it.

'This has been used twice,' I said, 'and the two sets of writing are superimposed. I have seen you extract information from blotters before, simply by reflecting them in a mirror, but surely this is more difficult?'

'Difficulty embraces the concept of success,' he said. 'It is completely distinguished from impossibility.'

He reached out for the paper and motioned me to join him in front of the mirror over our mantelpiece. He held up the blotting-paper so that both of us could see its reflection.

'But there you are!' I exclaimed. 'The two sets of lines are on top of each other.'

'So they are,' he agreed, 'but there is still much that may be read and who knows how much more that may be inferred. You will observe that there are fragments of an address at the top followed by what seems to be a greeting – "My -ear B" – let us hope that is "My dear Byron". Fortunately the good Doctor's penmanship is as bold as his choice of ink. He dips his pen with great frequency and a large amount of his text survives.

'Let us see,' he continued. 'We can discern "in person", then a gap, then "ence of", another gap, and "and -arde-s".'

'It does not signify much to me,' I said.

'Does it not, Watson? Surely this is Tumbletye saying to Byron that he would have seen him in person but for the presence of the Scotland Yarders, is it not?'

'This is all highly conjectural!' I exclaimed.

'So it may be, Watson, but it does not break the rules.'

'What rules?' I enquired.

'The immutable rules that govern logical deduction, Watson,' he snapped, 'and in particular the rule that any inference is permitted that neither distorts nor ignores the existing data.'

He turned back to the image in the mirror.

'There is a large area where the superimposition of the lines makes it impossible to discern any letters or words, then we have "avenge the wrong", a gap, and "oth Union and Empire". He is writing of some measure which will strike both Britain and the United States and avenge some real or imagined wrong against someone. Let me see, now there is "shame them", a blank and "old sod and our murdered country".'

He pondered for a moment then snapped his fingers. 'Of course! The old sod and their murdered country will be Ireland and the Confederate States. So Byron is an American, or at least one of those Britons who cast their lot with the Confederacy, and Tumbletye's plan to attack the Jubilee will be framed so as to speak both for the Irish cause and the Confederacy, but what does he require of Byron?'

He scrutinised the reflection again. 'More illegible blots, then "shamed by permitting the act", more space and then "by your participation". I do not fully understand this. He seems to be saying that Britain will be shamed by the act taking place here and, if I am right, that America will be shamed by Byron's involvement. Why should that be so?'

'Perhaps,' I suggested, 'Byron is an agent of Colonel Craig. Why, if some outrage were to occur at the Jubilee and the hand of the United States Government were discerned in it, it might lead us to war, Holmes!'

'I think not, Watson. If Byron were one of Craig's minions the Colonel would not need to have him discreetly protected and shadowed, he could simply warn and instruct him. No, there is some deep mystery surrounding our singular playwright, but it is not that. It seems to be more a question of who he is than what he is or was.'

'Perhaps he's really Jefferson Davis,' I joked.

'Watson!' protested Holmes. 'The first and only President of the Confederate States is at large in America and has been for many years, since he was acquitted of any part in the murder of Abraham Lincoln. He is not scribbling for a living in London.'

He stroked his chin. 'I could wish', he said, 'that Tumbletye was as slapdash in blotting his pages as he is in his writing and had not placed them so nearly on top of each other. Nevertheless, there is still more we can decipher. I see "you will not" followed later by "regardless". Can we safely conjecture that Tumbletye is saying that he will proceed whether Byron takes part or not? And with what, Watson? What is his plan?'

He fell silent and peered more intently at the mirror. Eventually he gave up and carried the paper to the window where he

91

pored over it with his lens. At last he dropped into a chair and sighed.

'There is little more that can be read and that little makes no sense,' he said. 'There are only small fragments and they appear to be "r-a-t", "o-w-e-l", "w-i-s" and the most mystifying of all – "zerod". If his scrawl were not so dramatic and his spacing even I might be able to estimate how many letters or spaces are missing but his scribble does not permit it.'

'What will you do, then?'

'I shall smoke a long pipe or two over the problem,' he said, reaching for the Persian slipper. 'I always find that there are few problems that do not reveal their solutions by the end of a third pipe at the most.'

I have long realised that I acted as a sounding board for my friend, against which he could throw his ideas until the echo of one of them made some sense to him. If by that means I was able to assist that great brain in wrestling with a puzzle I was content and it rarely crossed my mind to pit my wits against his finely tuned ratiocinative processes. Nevertheless, I have always been a great reader and, in that very summer, I was working on my first narrative of one of Holmes' cases. I believed that I knew a certain amount about words.

'They are all, except two, complete words,' I ventured. 'As to "o-w-e-l" it might be "towel" or "dowel" or "rowel".'

He looked at me with an expressionless stare. 'What, then, do you make of "z-e-r-o-d"?' he demanded.

A flash of inspiration came to me. 'Surely Tumbletye is an American – might it not be some American spelling that does not occur in correct English?' I ventured.

'Tumbletye's childhood was spent in Canada,' said Holmes. 'He will have been educated to write Imperial English not the American variety. What is more, I do not believe that even a madman like Tumbletye would find a use for the archaism "wis". May I bid you goodnight, Watson?'

I realised that my further presence would be superfluous and retired.

14

A STROLL IN THE PARK

I woke next morning fully expecting to find our sitting-room shrouded in tobacco smoke and was, therefore, surprised to find evidence that Mrs Hudson had been before me. Not only were the curtains drawn back and a window opened, but the cushions had been plumped, the table had been cleared and Holmes sat beside it in his dressing-gown, taking tea.

'Good morning, Watson,' he hailed me, and poured me a cup of tea.

'Have you', I asked as I seated myself, 'made any progress with the blotting-paper?'

'None, I fear,' he replied. 'However, if there was any doubt that the writing on it is Tumbletye's, that is now resolved.'

'Really?' I asked. 'How so?'

'This was delivered by hand early this morning.' He passed across a sheet of notepaper.

It was a heavy paper, bearing a deeply embossed heading which proclaimed Dr Tumbletye to be a 'Practitioner of Electric Medicine and Natural Healing'. A printed address in New York had been struck through and his Bloomsbury address written in followed by a short text, all in the lurid green ink which we had seen upon the blotter. It said:

I cannot prevent the fools at Scotland Yard from dogging my footsteps and interfering with my affairs but you Mr Holmes are a horse of another colour and you may be assured that I shall not allow you the same liberty.

If you continue to meddle with matters that do not concern you, I shall take appropriate measures.

I returned it to Holmes. 'A threat,' I remarked.

'I have seen many such,' he said, unruffled. 'It will do no harm to draw the mad Doctor's attention upon myself. It might encourage him to reveal his hand. You may observe that he spells "colour" in the English, rather than the American fashion.'

We had completed breakfast when Mrs Hudson announced Inspector Lestrade. The little detective's normally sallow complexion was a degree paler and dark shadows showed under his eyes.

'You have had a long night,' observed Holmes. 'Watson, be so kind as to ask Mrs Hudson for more coffee.'

Lestrade drank thirstily from the coffee when it arrived, then wiped his moustaches. 'I have, as you remark, Mr Holmes, had a long night. Chiefly on account of two cut-throats who you turned over to Sergeant Walters in Bloomsbury.'

Holmes sat forward. 'Have you succeeded in connecting them to the Thames corpses?' he asked.

The detective shook his head regretfully. 'No, Mr Holmes. The surgeon says that the knives are very likely the weapons that did the deed, but of course he can't be sure. We sweated them, Mr Holmes, believe you me, we sweated them in shifts, all night long but not a word of admission could we get out of them. To hear them speak you would think they were innocent passers-by who were arrested through no fault of their own.'

'Really?' said Holmes, sinking back into his chair. 'What account did they give of themselves?'

'They said that they was taking a stroll when a strange gentleman in a carriage asked for their help. He told them he had just drawn up outside his lodgings and had seen a lamp flash at his window. He believed he was being burgled. He told them there was no back way from his premises so they laid in wait for the burglars when they came out from the side of the house.'

'And how did they account for what followed?' asked my friend.

'When the burglars – that is, of course, yourself and the Doctor here – emerged, they set upon you, whereupon one was threatened with being shot and the other was beaten within an inch of his life.'

'Dear me, Watson,' said Holmes, 'I am surprised Lestrade has not called with a posse of constables to arrest us for house-breaking and assault.'

I chuckled, nervously, but Lestrade laughed. 'You haven't heard the half of it, gentlemen,' he said. 'They maintained that they was grateful to Sergeant Walters for arriving and rescuing them from two such bloodthirsty rogues, that they had never seen the knives until you showed them to the Sergeant and that the dark lantern and Jacob's Ladder was your equipment, not theirs. What do you make of that, Mr Holmes?'

'I do not suppose that they explained what business took two Whitechapel ruffians into Bloomsbury on a summer evening, did they, Lestrade?'

'No more they did, Mr Holmes. They insisted they was just walking about on a fine night.'

Holmes snorted. 'As likely a prospect as the idea that Watson and I would take an evening walk while armed with surgical knives and a pistol, not to mention being cluttered with a Jacob's Ladder and dark lantern. There is, however, one significant truth in their tale.'

'What's that, Mr Holmes?'

'The man in the carriage. There was certainly a carriage and though Watson and I never saw its occupant it is a reasonable inference that it was Tumbletye. The incident occurred within yards of his lodgings. I have recently obtained his address from an American journalist and Watson and I extended an evening walk to look at his place of abode.'

Lestrade nodded thoughtfully. 'You believe these men to be Tumbletye's minders,' he said, 'and that they attacked you at his command?'

'Indubitably,' said Holmes. 'Tumbletye would have been shocked to see me in the vicinity of his lodgings and reacted by setting his bullies on us. What do you propose to do with them?'

'We cannot lay the murders to their charge,' said the police officer, 'but we shall charge them with intent to commit burglary. They will have a job explaining the Jacob's Ladder.'

'So they will,' said my friend, 'but I suggest that while you have them in custody you search their lodgings. They may be cut-throats now but they will have risen from the ranks of petty thieves and you may well find something that will connect them to the dead men in the river.'

'Indeed,' said Lestrade, 'a good idea, Mr Holmes. I shall set about that now.'

He took his leave of us and Holmes showed him out with a smile.

'Well, Watson,' he said, as the door closed behind Lestrade, 'it seems we have escaped the law.'

'So we have,' I chuckled. 'It is as well that Lestrade places no belief in anything Tumbletye's men have said.'

'It is as well', said Holmes, 'that Lestrade applies not the least touch of logic in his enquiries, or he might wonder why Tumbletye should connect me in any way with his affairs. Until last night there was no connection which Tumbletye might have perceived.'

He settled down again at the table with his piece of blotting-paper and I stepped over to the window. If Holmes was about to go into one of his reveries over the paper, it would be immaterial to him whether I was there or not and I had it in mind to evade the fug of his pipe by taking a stroll.

As though reading my mind Holmes asked, 'Are you going out, Watson?'

'It is a fair day,' I said, 'and you seem to be deeply involved with Tumbletye's letter. I thought I might leave you to your examination of it.'

'Watson,' he said, 'if I was ungrateful for your suggestions last night, I am sorry. I am sure you now recognise that we are not dealing with American spelling nor, most probably, with archaisms and I recognise that you offered the suggestion in order to assist me.'

I was almost speechless. In the six years of our acquaintance I had often known the rough edge of his tongue when I ventured what appeared to me as perfectly reasonable suggestions, but rarely did he acknowledge them afterwards, let alone apologise.

'That's perfectly all right, Holmes,' I stammered, 'On reflection I have realised that "wis" is probably not the word he used. Are you sure you have read the letters correctly?'

'As sure as I may be,' he said. 'The proof that Tumbletye is not a properly qualified doctor seems to lie in the bold clarity of his script.'

'Well,' I said, 'I really have no further ideas on the subject. Perhaps it would be as well if I left you to your consideration of the problem.'

'Not at all,' he cried, 'not at all. Pray assist me by your presence, Watson. The occasional exchange of observations between us has often been of use in clarifying my thoughts.'

He extended the Persian slipper towards me. 'Here,' he invited, 'be a good fellow, fill your pipe and settle down in the basket chair. It will be of considerable assistance to me to know that you are there if I wish to argue through a chain of thought that occurs to me.'

I had never known my friend so earnest in seeking my company and I admit that I was flattered. I stuffed my pipe, made myself comfortable in the basket chair and started to read a magazine. Holmes stretched himself at length upon the couch, minutely examining the blotting-paper with his lens.

The hours passed in silence. Not one word did Holmes utter. Instead he dropped the blotting-paper to the floor, cast his head back on the cushions and closed his eyes, so that it was impossible to be sure that he was not asleep.

Mrs Hudson brought us luncheon, but Holmes merely pecked at his food and answered my few questions in an abstracted fashion, which revealed to me that he had seen no answer to the problem of the blotting-paper.

Holmes required no dinner and the thick tobacco fug which had built up in our little sitting-room reduced my appetite so that I dined upon a sandwich and returned to my post in the basket chair. I had no idea what variation of his method Holmes was applying, but I found it decidedly dull.

At length I consulted my watch and concluded that it was time for bed. I remarked so to Holmes, who opened his eyes, drew out his watch and stared at it.

'I had no idea that so much time had elapsed,' he remarked. Twisting his long frame off the couch he stepped to the window and gazed down into the street for several seconds.

'Yes, Watson,' he said as he turned back from the window, 'you must take your rest, of course, but I shall try a little longer to extract meaning from Tumbletye's fragments,' with which he bade me an affable goodnight and composed himself upon the couch once more.

The next day followed suit. I sat in the basket chair, rereading magazines and trying not to look at my watch, while Holmes sprawled silently along the couch, only the fumes of his pipe showing that he was awake. From time to time he would rise, stretch himself, and glance out of the window, but still he vouchsafed me no indication of his train of thought. If, indeed, my presence was useful to him in any way it did not seem to be bearing results.

It was early evening when he swung his long legs to the floor and made another visit to the window.

'It is a pleasant evening, Watson,' he remarked, 'and you have sat by me loyally while I have addressed barely a word to you for a day and a half. Pray ring for our boots and let us take the air.'

I was further confused. Despite his athletic abilities, Holmes never took exercise for its own sake and he seemed to be totally impervious to the mephitic atmosphere bred by his long sessions of meditation over his pipe.

Nevertheless in five minutes we were on the pavement, making our way at a leisurely pace towards the gate of the park.

It was, as Holmes had remarked, a pleasant evening and, after strolling awhile by the water, we took seats and watched the swans gliding past us. The air was warm, and from behind us a slight breeze carried the fragrance of some flowering tree. There seemed to be an underlying sharpness in the scent that was familiar but I could not name it. Oddly, I found myself reminded of my training days at the Military Hospital at Netley.

I was about to ask Holmes' advice as to the perfume when something cold and narrow pressed against my neck on the right side and a heavy hand fell on my left shoulder.

'Don't move, Doctor,' hissed a rough voice, 'or I 'll slit your wizand,' and I heard the same command given to Holmes by a second voice.

A moment later a cloth pad was thrust into my face and, as darkness descended on me, I realised that the perfume of the shrubs had concealed the scent of chloroform.

15

A VISIT FROM THE DOCTOR

I was not, at first, certain that I had really recovered consciousness. As my senses returned I attempted to open my eyes, but they seemed almost glued shut. My head pounded and my mouth was dry. I tried to move only to discover that I was fixed in an extremely uncomfortable position. I lay on something hard and my arms were firmly trapped behind my back.

For a little time I remained still, trying to recruit my strength. The smell of chloroform was still strong, but was now mixed with other smells, principally cheap disinfectant and strong soap, though these failed to disguise the presence of less wholesome odours.

At last I felt that my tongue might function and I croaked Holmes' name.

'Here, Watson,' he replied cheerily and I could tell that he was close to me and at the same level. 'You may open your eyes,' he continued.

I did so and the light, though dull, struck painfully on my eyeballs. Gradually I focused on my surroundings.

Holmes and I lay close together on the stone floor of a square room. We were strapped into canvas jackets, the arms of which were secured behind our backs by heavy leather straps. Around us the walls of the room were of plain stone and only a small, high window of thick glass, heavily barred, lit the place. Along each side of the room ran a thick plank shelf.

'We are in a cell!' I gasped.

'More accurately, Watson,' said Holmes, 'we are in a room of St Muriel's Home for the Bewildered, somewhere in the vicinity of Hampstead, I think.'

'You can identify it?' I asked.

'I was rather expecting the chloroform attack and my studies in the Japanese martial arts have trained me to control my

100

breathing to a large extent. As a result I was not so severely affected by the drug as you have been, Watson. While feigning unconsciousness I was able to observe our destination.'

'But what is it all about?' I demanded.

'I fear you will berate me for leading you unknowingly into danger again, Watson, but I had really no other course. When Tumbletye threatened me in his note, I determined to draw him out, and I have done so. By remaining at home we forced him to come and seek us out.'

'But he might have had his thugs kill us!' I exclaimed.

'Not he,' said Holmes, with assurance. 'His business is his plot against the Jubilee. He is not so mad as not to realise that my disappearance would cause unhealthy excitement at Scotland Yard, who are already dogging his footsteps. No, he has merely, as he believes, removed us from the board while he completes his plan. He might, however, feel it expedient to dispose of us after the Jubilee.'

Holmes seemed unruffled by that prospect, but I cannot say that I was content to find myself the helpless prisoner of a homicidal lunatic.

'The Jubilee is now very close,' I pointed out.

'Precisely, Watson, and I was making little headway in elucidating Tumbletye's plans. For that very reason it was necessary for me to come face to face with him in circumstances where he believes that he has the upper hand. In that way I may persuade him to reveal his intentions, after which we shall be able to take steps to foil his plot.'

'If we can escape from here,' I remarked.

'That, Watson, is the least of our problems,' he said, with such confidence that I could only assume that he knew what he was doing.

How long we lay I do not know. Some time later I heard bolts being drawn on the outside of our door, then the door was flung open and three men entered.

Two were ruffians of the kind that Holmes and I had encountered in Bloomsbury, though not clad now in the raffish finery of their kind but in dark uniforms with peaked caps. Each had a holstered pistol at his belt and a short club in his hand.

Between them stood one of the most curious individuals I have ever seen. He was a man of over six feet, loosely built and big-boned, and his excessive size was exaggerated by his dramatic dress. He wore a plum-coloured velvet tunic, heavily frogged with gold cord and richly decorated with braid at the cuffs and shoulders. Beneath the jacket were white riding trousers with broad stripes of gold down their sides and these disappeared into polished black boots that came up mid-thigh.

His long, narrow face was pale and showed two wide, watery eyes, a pendulous nose and the most extraordinary moustache I had seen in years. It swept away from both sides of his upper lip, hanging in great tufts down either side of his jaw, and was trimmed away at its centre to expose his small, fleshy mouth. Like his hair the moustache was naturally grey but had been died a lurid yellow. This could be none other than the American Doctor.

He stood and surveyed us for a moment, then dismissed the two guards, telling them to wait outside.

'Now,' he said, 'let me introduce myself, gentlemen. I am Dr Francis J. Tumbletye, practitioner of electric and Indian medicine, Knight of the Golden Circle of the Confederacy and an Invincible of the Fenian Brotherhood.'

His voice was high-pitched, with a Canadian drawl.

'In other words,' I said, 'a practitioner of quackery, a former spy for a nation that no longer exists and a member of a gang of cut-throats.'

He laughed. 'Another time will have to do for us to dispute the virtues of electric medicine, Doctor. I am here as the representative of two nations that have a very real existence – the Confederate States of America and the Independent Republic of Ireland.'

'I had thought', said Holmes, 'that the Confederate States surrendered and that Ireland was a province of the British Empire.'

Tumbletye laughed again. 'Oh, you English!' he exclaimed. 'You always believe that you can destroy ideas with steel and gunpowder, that you can trample other people's freedom in the dirt with the boots of your redcoats. The Americans have become just like you since they fought and beat you. The

102

Confederacy wanted no war, merely to go about its own ways, and for that Lincoln's armies burned their way to the sea. But the Confederacy was and is an ideal in the hearts of men, as is an independent Ireland. I am here to see that those dreams are brought to the world's notice in such a fashion that the British Empire and the so-called United States will never be able to hold up their damned flags again.'

'What have you got against Britain and the Union?' asked my friend.

'What have I got, Mr Holmes? Hatred, that's what. Hatred of the English because they have stolen my native country and oppressed its people for centuries! Hatred of the Union because it destroyed my adopted country! When I have finished, Mr Holmes, there will be no Jubilee. I shall strike such a blow on the very eve of the Jubilee that Victoria will go in mourning to church, not in celebration. Britain will be damned in the eyes of her allies and the whole world and America with her. You shall see!'

'An ambitious programme,' remarked Holmes. 'Do you not think that Scotland Yard may have something to say on the subject?'

'Scotland Yard!' laughed Tumbletye. 'You yourself have never been among their greatest admirers, I believe. What can they do? Littlechild orders his men to follow me about London because he knows why I am here, but he knows no more and he cannot prevent my plan from succeeding. No, Mr Holmes, I pay you the compliment of believing you to be a far more serious danger to my plans. That is why I have had to bring you here.'

'You do me too great an honour, Doctor,' said Holmes. 'Would it not have been as easy to dispose of Watson and me in Regent's Park, as your colleagues cut down Burke and Cavendish in Dublin?'

'I am a patriot, not a murderer,' said Tumbletye. 'Burke died because he was an Irishman and a traitor to his fellow countrymen. Cavendish would not have died if he had not intervened. You and the Doctor are English and I cannot fault you for pursuing what you believe to be the interests of your country. You will merely be my guests until my plan is complete. I regret that I could not give you softer lodgings, but I did not wish to

103

tempt your considerable ingenuity into devising ways of escape. Then I should have to kill you. As it is, you may suffer a certain amount of discomfort but I shall arrange your release in due course.'

'You are too kind, Doctor,' said Holmes. 'Tell me, what is Byron's part in all this?'

'Byron,' said Tumbletye, 'if he will play his part, will help me to show the world that Britain is corrupt and lazy, more concerned with shows than reality, and that the Union is founded on falsehoods, that it tells whatever lies serve its greedy cause. You and the world will learn about Byron in due course.'

He stepped to the door. 'I shall have my men bring you some food but I fear you cannot be released from the strait-jackets. Goodnight, gentlemen,' and he was gone.

'Well,' I exploded, 'he is everything that Lestrade said and more – an absolute madman!'

'Oh, indeed,' agreed Holmes, 'but that does not mean he cannot put his insane plans into operation. If he is really the brains behind the Invincibles then he has done considerable harm already without Littlechild making a case against him.'

'And what are we going to do, Holmes? Surely we cannot stay here while that lunatic attacks the Queen?'

'He does not, apparently, intend to attack the Queen. He says that she will still go to church on Jubilee Day but to mourn. He has something else in mind. As to our course of action, Watson, I believe we should sample the house cuisine and then consider bidding our farewells to St Muriel's.'

'But have you already learned enough from Tumbletye?'

'I have learned as much as he is willing to reveal, and it may be enough for my purposes.'

16

A VIGOROUS FAREWELL

In military and civilian life I have known some hard lying, but little that matches the discomfort I experienced as Tumbletye's prisoner. The canvas jackets were tightly fitted and permitted little movement once the straps were buckled.

We had some small relief when a guard brought us our supper. He unstrapped one of our arms to enable us to eat and drink, but only one of us at a time was permitted even this degree of freedom and I could not see how Holmes proposed we should escape.

Holmes lingered over his food, chatting amiably with the guard.

'You seem to take the most elaborate precautions,' he remarked.

The guard laughed. 'People who come here are sent because someone doesn't want 'em somewhere else,' he said. 'They pay us well to see that they won't be embarrassed by relatives who have taken a funny turn. It wouldn't do at all if we was to be letting them walk out now, would it?'

'I imagine not,' said Holmes, 'but it seems to me that anyone with sufficient strength or skill to escape from these jackets could find a way out.'

'I've been here twelve years,' said our keeper, 'and no one has ever got free of them jackets. And if they did, what would they do? We're all armed, you know,' and he tapped his pistol holster. 'Besides,' he continued, 'the grounds are walled, there are dogs in the house and we've a direct telegraph to the police. I can't see anyone getting very far, so I should put it out of your mind if I was you.'

'Oh, I was not contemplating an escape,' said Holmes. 'It was merely curiosity. Perhaps you could tell me one more thing – do you know why Dr Tumbletye has brought us here?'

The guard chuckled. 'He says as you and your friend believe that you are Mr Sherlock Holmes and Dr Watson and that you have a mission to save Her Majesty from a Fenian outrage. He says your family has paid to have you out of the way until the Jubilee is over so as you won't cause Her Majesty any embarrassment. If I was you, I would behave yourself for a day or two and that'll be it – you'll be let go, none the worse for it.'

He collected our rubber dishes and wooden spoons and left, wishing us goodnight and reminding us that breakfast was at seven. Once the door was closed we heard heavy bolts being slid into place on the other side.

'It is impossible, Holmes,' I said when I was sure that the guard was gone. 'There is no way out of this place. You heard what he said.'

'Our attendant', said Holmes, 'has been kind enough to tell us what he knows. A man's beliefs are shaped by what he knows and I believe escape is possible because I know more than our friend. Now if breakfast is not until seven, I suggest that we try to sleep.'

'But surely the night is the best time to attempt an escape!' I said.

'A common belief,' he replied, 'and for that reason they will expect it. In addition, there will be fewer persons about this building at night and we shall be the more easily seen. No, Watson, it is time to take such rest as we can.'

I rested little. Apart from the cramping discomfort of our restraints, darkness brought forth a dismal, persistent wailing cry from the occupant of the next room, soon answered by others throughout the building. Even in physical ease I would have found it difficult to sleep while those poor wretches howled in their mad loneliness around us. So I dozed fitfully, thanking my fate that at worst I must only experience a few days of this misery.

At last a faint blue tinged the high window of our cell and Holmes hissed, 'Watson! Are you awake?'

'I do not think I've been anything else all night,' I complained.

'A pity,' he commented, 'for we shall need our wits about us.'

'You have a plan?' I asked.

'You do me less than justice, Watson! I have always had a plan. Can you position yourself so that your hands are close to my boots?'

I humped myself round on the floor, my confined muscles screaming at every move, and eventually reached a position where I could touch Holmes' boot heels.

'Can you identify my right boot heel by touch?' he asked.

With the limited movement of my fingers permitted by the strait-jacket I managed to grasp what I believed was his right heel.

'I have it,' I reported.

'Excellent,' he said. 'Now twist it slowly for ninety degrees in a clockwise direction.'

I did as he asked and was surprised to find that the entire heel rotated under my fingers.

'Feel carefully underneath it,' said Holmes, 'and you will find a useful implement.'

Cautiously I felt the part of the sole uncovered when I had moved the heel. My fingers touched something smooth and metallic and I pried it out of its cavity as Holmes said, 'Be sure that you do not drop it, Watson.'

Soon I knew that my fingers held a small but very sharp blade. By repositioning myself against Holmes' back I was able to cut the straps that held his arms. It was not very long before he was free and soon after he unstrapped me.

'Do you always carry that blade?' I asked.

'Only when I believe it may be required,' he said. 'There lies the advantage of persuading Tumbletye to believe that he had caught us unawares. It has not crossed his mind that I decided when we should be captured and was, accordingly, prepared.'

We sat and massaged our cramped and aching limbs while he outlined the first stages of his plan to me. Gradually the light grew in the window and at last we heard a guard moving along the corridor outside, drawing the bolts of each room in turn and feeding each inmate.

When the guard reached our neighbour Holmes motioned me to take up my position. I lay on the floor, clad in the strait-jacket and trying to look as if it had not been disturbed.

The door of the next cell was closed and soon we heard our bolts being drawn. My friend took up a position behind the door. As the guard entered, with a rubber dish of porridge in each hand, he suddenly realised that Holmes was no longer lying on the floor. With a muttered ejaculation he turned, but it was too late.

Holmes' hand moved out of the shadows behind the door, faster than a striking snake. He seemed barely to touch the man's neck, but the guard slumped to the floor silently.

Quickly I donned the guard's uniform, while my friend bound and gagged the unconscious man with strips cut from one of the strait-jackets.

Holmes pulled on the other strait-jacket and together we left the room, bolting it behind us. To our left the corridor was a dead end so we made our way in the opposite direction, trying to present the appearance of a guard escorting a patient. It seemed to work for we passed another uniformed guard who took no notice of us.

We had reached the corridor's end, where it opened on to a landing around a square stairwell, when there came a shout from behind us. Glancing back I saw the guard we had passed with his colleague whom we had left trussed. As I watched they reached a lever on the wall and one of them jerked it down, causing alarm bells to ring throughout the building.

'Where to, Holmes?' I asked.

He threw off the strait-jacket and glanced over the rail to the floor, two storeys below. More uniforms were appearing below us and beginning to run up the stairs.

'Up seems to be the only sensible option,' he declared and sprang for the upper staircase. As we reached the top of the stairs, a crowd of guards reached the bottom and a bullet ricocheted up the stairs.

'Quickly, Watson!' commanded Holmes and dragged me aside into a small doorway. Lifting his foot he kicked vigorously at the door which burst open to let us stumble through into the open air.

We were on the roof of the asylum, in a square and level area the centre of which was the roof light for the stairwell.

108

Holmes pointed to two large brick constructions alongside the roof light.

'Water tanks,' he said. 'Be so good as to take a position behind one and hold the pursuit at bay while I examine possible means of escape.'

I ran to the rear of one of the big brick cubes and, as the first guards emerged from the stair door, put a shot across their heads. They withdrew for a moment then a pistol barrel poked around the door and a shot whistled past me.

Holmes was back at my side. 'Is there a way down?' I asked.

'Only one,' he said, 'and it is a little risky, but it has the advantage of being concealed from our pursuers.'

He pointed behind us. I could see nothing except the low parapet that surrounded the roof and two wires attached to china insulators which were, I imagined, the telegraph of which our guard had spoken.

'How shall we do it?' I asked.

'By telegraph,' said Holmes. 'Give them another shot to discourage them, but be careful. We may need ammunition to cope with the dogs.'

I placed another shot close to the stair door and drew two more in reply.

'Now,' said Holmes, 'they believe that they have us trapped up here. They will be content to keep us here until we have exhausted our ammunition before they venture on to the roof. That should give us time to make our exit.'

He stepped to the parapet and took from his pocket a handkerchief and his little blade. Wrapping the cloth around his hand he took hold of one of the telegraph wires and began to hack it away from its insulator with the blade. In a few strokes he had freed it and he passed me the blade and told me to do the same with the other wire.

As I did so I said, 'But surely these wires will not support our weight!'

'They do not need to,' he said. 'They merely need to give us a certain degree of direction. Look,' he said, pointing across the parapet, 'do you see how both wires pass across and through the branches of that tree on the lawns? We shall travel a little fast

109

and I suggest that we draw our knees up, but I do not think we shall come to much harm.'

With which confident observation he took a firm grip with both hands on the wire and stepped over the parapet. Summoning as much nerve as I could muster, I followed him two seconds later.

17

THE AMERICAN DIMENSION

If I had been allowed the time to reflect, it might have occurred to me that Holmes and I would have been better off in our cell than leaping from a rooftop on a purely theoretical conjecture, but no sooner had my feet left the parapet than I found myself hurtling downwards, convinced that I would crash to the ground, three storeys below, sustaining serious injuries at the very least.

I was therefore surprised when I found that the wire which I clutched was pulling me away from the building and towards the great oak tree a few feet away, over the branches of which both wires passed.

I was moving at alarming speed, but the branches of the oak suddenly took up the slack of the wire with a series of bouncing jolts, which very nearly detached my grip. A second later I found myself hurtling under the shadow of the tree, the grass very close beneath me and passing at high speed.

I recalled Holmes' warning to keep my feet up, and attempted to do so. I caught a glimpse of him rocketing through the air ahead of me and heard him cry, 'Let go, Watson, or you will swing back!'

I do not know if I would have possessed sufficient nerve to relinquish my hold on the cable, but the choice was, in every sense, taken out of my hands. Another great jerk emanated from the tree, separating me from the wire and depositing me violently on the lawn, across which I slid and tumbled for some distance before coming to rest in a heap at the very feet of my friend.

He had no sooner helped me up than he was sprinting across the lawn towards the perimeter wall. As I made after him I heard the cry of dogs behind. I cast a hurried glance over my shoulder and saw three large, dark shapes pounding across the sward, baying as they came.

I knew that I could not outrun them but Holmes might well do so if I managed to delay the brutes. I whirled, pulled the guard's pistol from its holster, and fired at the leading animal. I have no desire to brag, but I believe that my time in the Army made me a reasonably proficient shot. Shaken and breathless as I was, I was pleased to see the dog fall with a pained yelp.

My second shot went wide and the remaining animals were rapidly closing on me. The third shot struck the second dog, after which the pistol's hammer fell on an empty chamber. I took the weapon by its butt and prepared to grapple with the remaining hound but to my relief it seemed disheartened by the fate of its comrades. It abandoned the chase, turning aside and retreating towards the asylum building.

'Quick, Watson!' called Holmes. I turned to see him astride the wall, reaching down to assist me. Moments later we both tumbled down the outside of the wall into a patch of scrub in a narrow lane.

We jogged downhill and soon found ourselves, as Holmes had predicted, on the outskirts of Hampstead where we were able to find a cab to carry us home to Baker Street. Poor Mrs Hudson had become well used, over the years, to Holmes' arrivals in a wide variety of guises, but my appearance in the character of an asylum guard caused her grave misgivings. 'It's all very well for Mr Holmes,' she remarked within my earshot, 'for he's a consulting detective, but I don't believe that a doctor should be going about pretending to be what he isn't.'

Nevertheless, she spread an excellent breakfast before us and told us that John Essex had called several times to see if we were there. Holmes telegraphed the reporter at the Green Dragon and almost before we had completed our meal the American was being shown in.

'Mr Holmes, Doctor, where have you been?' he asked before he had sat down. 'I was beginning to believe that Tumbletye had done away with you.'

Holmes chuckled. 'Watson and I have been enjoying a little of Dr Tumbletye's hospitality,' he said, 'in the course of which he assured us that he had no desire to harm us.'

Quickly he gave Essex an outline of our adventures in Hampstead.

'Tarnation!' exclaimed the journalist after Holmes' recital. 'I guess you'd rather have stayed one night than two! But did you find out anything?'

'We established that his plot is not directed against Her Majesty's person, but rather against the Throne as an institution. He spoke of her going to church on Jubilee Day to mourn, not to celebrate.'

'Then is he going to strike at some other member of her family?' asked Essex.

'He also ranted about shaming both the United States and the British Empire in the eyes of the world,' said Holmes. 'If it is a simple assassination that he plans – even of a member of the royal family – that would surely attract sympathy for the victim's country and condemnation of the perpetrators. Even the Fenians have left the royal family alone, though it would be easy enough to attack them if they wished. Only madmen attack royalty in this country. No, I think it is not simply an assassination, it is some kind of symbolic gesture.'

'Tumbletye is a madman,' I pointed out.

'True, Watson, but you heard him indicate that Her Majesty would survive whatever he plans.'

'So,' said Essex, 'we know what he won't do but we don't know what he will do. Did he give you any indication of where or when?'

'Only that he intends to strike on the eve of the Jubilee,' said Holmes, 'so that the celebration will be marred from the outset by his demonstration. That is tomorrow, gentlemen, so we have little time.'

'But now we know where and when!' declared Essex, triumphantly.

'Really?' said Holmes.

'Oh yes,' said the reporter. 'The Court Circular gives Her Majesty only one appointment tomorrow. She was so impressed by her visit to the Wild West Show that she has commanded Colonel Cody to give a performance for her guests at Windsor tomorrow. That must be the target!'

'Of course,' said Holmes. 'A relaxed gathering of two-thirds of the royalty of Europe and many politicians to enjoy a huge and spectacular entertainment – what opportunities there will be for

113

Tumbletye at Windsor! And he did tell us, Watson – he did tell us. Do you not recall that he spoke of the Empire being corrupt and lazy? "More concerned with shows than reality" were his words. And the presence of Cody's entirely American show confirms it – the American dimension. You are right, Mr Essex. He intends to inflict his own distorted reality on the Queen's entertainment at Windsor!'

'But what does he intend to do?' I asked.

'Perhaps a bomb outrage aimed at the gathering. That would achieve what he threatened,' said my friend. 'If visiting royalty and diplomats were killed or injured it would certainly destroy Her Majesty's celebration. Be so kind as to ring for Mrs Hudson, will you, Watson?'

He dashed off a telegram, asked our landlady to replenish the coffee, and sat back in the basket chair.

'Now,' he said to Essex, 'you have discovered something yourself?'

'I have indeed,' said the American. 'You remember how Byron attacked Candover at the theatre? Well, I have been looking into Mr Candover's past.'

'And what have you found?' asked Holmes.

'Some very strange things,' said Essex. 'Firstly Candover is not his real name – it is Dunham. Secondly he was almost certainly a spy in the Civil War.'

'For which interest?' asked Holmes.

'A good question,' said Essex. 'One story says he is a Southerner who never fought against the Union and went north towards the end of the war; another says he is a New Yorker who lived in the South and was drafted into their army, later going north. It seems he has told both tales himself.'

'And what do you think?' said Holmes.

'My best contact says that, wherever he was born, Candover was a double agent during the war, only becoming a Union agent when it was plain that the South had lost. Then he became an important tool of the War Department.'

'In what way?'

'After President Lincoln was assassinated, the War Department issued a proclamation saying that the Confederate President Jefferson Davis and members of his cabinet were parties to the plot to kill Lincoln. They declared a reward of one hundred thousand dollars for Davis and he was captured, but they charged him only with treason, not with Lincoln's murder.'

'I followed your Civil War closely as a boy,' I said. 'Surely there was a strong movement to execute Davis?'

He nodded. 'There was indeed, and the House of Representatives asked the War Department what was the evidence against Davis. They wanted to hang Davis and, if they could, connect President Johnson with the plot so that they could impeach him, but it all blew up in their faces.'

'In what manner?' enquired Holmes.

'A Senator Rogers from New Jersey got suspicious of the Department's witnesses and started checking on their backgrounds. He blew them apart one after another – proved they were liars, criminals, paid informers – but Candover was the worst of the lot. Rogers proved that he had given perjured evidence at Davis's trial and that Candover was running a school for witnesses in the National Hotel where he wrote out the evidence they were to give and rehearsed them over and over again.'

'And were no steps taken against him?' I asked.

'Surely. He was confronted by the Judiciary Committee of the House, but said that his witnesses had been bought by Davis's friends. He asked to be allowed to go to New York so he could prove it. They fell for it and let him go, but he jumped his escort and disappeared. Eventually they captured him and he got ten years in Albany Penitentiary for perjury. That is the man that Byron attacked.'

Holmes steepled his fingers before his face. 'That is most interesting, Mr Essex,' he said, after a pause, 'but it would be a great deal more interesting if you would vouchsafe us your confidence and tell us what you know or believe about Byron.'

'I have told you, Mr Holmes. I cannot do that – not out of loyalty to the United States and not out of fear of Colonel Craig.'

'Very well,' said Holmes. 'I have asked you twice and you have refused. Let us leave the matter. What do you make of this?' and he passed Essex the blotting-paper.

'That is Tumbletye's hand,' said the reporter. 'Where did it come from?'

'I too have my secrets,' smiled Holmes and went on to outline his ideas as to the content of the document.

Essex held it up to the mirror for a short while then gave it back to Holmes. With a wry grin he remarked, 'With that list of names you surely do not need me to tell you about Byron?'

'List of names!' exclaimed Holmes and snatched the paper from the reporter's hand. He pulled out his pocket-book and fumbled for the much-worn newspaper cutting which described Byron's attack on Candover.

He read fragments aloud: ' "... a strangely dressed old man who had something of the aspect of an Old Testament prophet... uttered cries of 'Ashtaroth! What did you do to Ashtaroth?' and 'Herod! Poor innocent Herod! Their blood is upon you and that of Mary who died dreadfully for nothing! Holy innocents! Holy innocents! You drove John out of Egypt and when he knew of her fate he wept and vowed vengeance. Oh, poor Sohrab, poor Sohrab!' " '

Holmes turned again to the blotting-paper. 'Z-e-r-o-d,' he recited and smote his brow with his fist. 'Of course! Not Ashtaroth, but Atzerodt! – "What did you do to Atzerodt?" – and the others will be the same. Herod must be Herold. Mary and John are Mary and John Surrat, not Sohrab, and they were not "Holy Innocents", but "wholly innocent"...'

He stopped suddenly, leaving me entirely confused. His new reading of the cutting made no more sense than the original to me. He stared intently at the blotting-paper, then snapped his fingers.

'W-i-s!' he exclaimed. 'Lewis, who was known as Paine! Am I right, Mr Essex?'

The American smiled wryly again. 'I do believe that you have it, Mr Holmes.'

Holmes swung to me. 'Now that I know who Byron is, I understand his intended part in Tumbletye's plot, Watson. Be so good as to summon a cab. We must see Byron straightaway.'

'But what of your telegram, and who is Byron?' I asked.

'The telegram was to Lestrade. His answer will be either "yes" or "no" – either can wait,' he snapped. 'As to Byron, I suggest you consider his broken ankle, Watson.'

18

THE MARK OF CAIN

We were not many minutes in reaching Byron's lodgings but his landlady informed us that he was at the British Museum for the day. We pursued him there and soon spotted him in the great Reading Room.

The playwright looked up in alarm as we gathered around him.

'Mr Holmes!' he exclaimed in a whisper. 'What brings you here?'

'An urgent question, Mr Byron, as to Dr Tumbletye's intentions,' replied Holmes.

Byron shook his silver head. 'I know nothing of Tumbletye's intentions,' he said. 'I have told you – I wish nothing to do with that man,' and he turned back to his books.

'Mr Byron,' whispered Holmes, a little louder, 'I do not expect you to have to do with Tumbletye, but I do require you to tell me about his letter.'

Byron swung back and stared at Holmes, his black eyes starting in his pale face.

'What letter?' he hissed. 'There has been no letter.'

'Tumbletye wrote to you, urging you to assist his scheme on behalf of the Fenians and the Confederacy, Mr Byron,' said my friend. His voice had risen again, drawing the attention of one or two other occupants of the Reading Room, some of whom directed reproving glances at us.

'I have nothing to say to you, Mr Holmes, and you are making a scene,' said Byron.

'Then I suggest that we step outside and you tell me what you know,' said Holmes, louder yet, 'before we are invited to leave by the Museum's staff.'

Byron cast a hunted look around him, observing that several of his fellow readers were now looking at us. He groaned, closed his book and stood up.

'Very well,' he whispered and dropping his head with an air of weary resignation he picked up his silver-headed stick and limped towards the doors.

Out in the Museum's sunlit courtyard he flung himself on to a bench. He looked defeated, gazing up at Sherlock Holmes with a look of fearful expectation.

'What is it you wish to know, Mr Holmes?' he asked.

'Firstly,' said Holmes, 'why you have tried to conceal from me your true identity.'

Byron lowered his head again, and swung it slowly from side to side.

'I cannot see,' he said, 'that my identity matters to you.'

'It seems to matter very much to Colonel Pericles Craig,' remarked Holmes.

Byron started. 'Craig!' he exclaimed. 'Craig knows I am here?'

'It was Craig's men,' said Holmes, 'who followed you about. He had sent them, it seems, to protect you from Tumbletye. Both of them died at the hands of Tumbletye's thugs.'

'Tumbletye killed them!' said Byron.

Holmes nodded. 'And, if you do not take part in his plot, he will do the same to you. On the other hand, if you play the part he expects, he will betray you.'

'Betray me?' repeated Byron. 'Why should Tumbletye betray me if I assist him? We are both...' and he fell silent.

'You are, or you were, both Knights of the Golden Circle,' said Holmes, causing Byron to start again, 'but he will not hesitate to betray. It is a part of his design.'

Byron shook his head again. 'It cannot be,' he said.

'But it is,' insisted Holmes. 'Tumbletye proposes a major outrage on the eve of the Jubilee – one that will shame both Britain and the United States. If he succeeds, Britain may be shamed by the fact of his success, but to drag the United States into it he needs to show the world that the perpetrator of the outrage was a man that the United States has declared to be dead for more than twenty years – a Confederate doing duty upon his own responsibility – John Wilkes Booth, the assassin of Abraham Lincoln!'

My mind whirled. Holmes was saying that the crippled playwright huddled on the bench was Booth, yet John Wilkes Booth had been shot dead by the Union Army and his co-conspirators hanged or imprisoned. How could Booth be alive and in our presence?

Byron lifted his face and it bore an expression of the deepest pain.

'Since you know so much, Mr Holmes, what more is there that I can tell you?'

'You can tell me,' said Holmes, 'as my client, how you come to be here in London and why you attacked Candover. Then, as a man who has no grievance against our Queen, you can tell me what Tumbletye plans and help me to foil his plot.'

Byron was silent for long moments, then he said, 'Very well, Mr Holmes. I will tell you what I can.'

He shuddered and drew his cape around him. 'I am a Virginian,' he said. 'Oh, my father was from Sheffield, but I was born in Virginia and when my native state left the Union, when the Union invaded us, I desired nothing better than to lay down my life for my state. But it was not to be. My mother made me swear an oath that I would not enlist for the Confederacy.'

He paused. 'So I continued in my profession. I was feted as a star while my fellow countrymen suffered hardship and death for the cause; while they died I was applauded night after night, received in the best circles of the Union, showered with money. Night after night I listened to the ladies of Union society and their menfolk crowing over their tables about what they would do to the Confederacy. Can you imagine how I felt?'

We nodded.

'I knew that I must do something for my country,' he continued. 'Oh, I paid out huge sums to buy medical aids for the Confederacy, I carried information to and from our intelligence service in Canada, but the war flowed against us and it seemed only a matter of time before we would be forced to grovel to the Union and submit to all those plans I had heard described with loving detail over supper tables in Washington. I knew that I must do more.'

He shuddered again. 'I formed a plan together with a few trusted friends, a plan to kidnap Lincoln and hold him hostage while the Confederacy negotiated peace on terms that would permit it to survive. We tried once, but our plan miscarried.

'Time was running out. Our armies were short of supplies, the Union was making headway against us. It was then that Candover approached me.'

'Aah!' breathed Holmes as though he had been expecting this.

'He put himself forward as a brother of the Golden Circle. He agreed with me that time was short and he said that he could help us. He said that he had connections in the Union, important connections, men who sympathised with us. What we must do, he said, was not kidnap Lincoln, but kill him and others.'

He stopped and rocked on his seat as if in pain. 'And, like a fool, I believed him. It had never been my intent to shed Lincoln's blood, but the agony of my dying country, the failure of our kidnap plan, the collapse of our armies, all beat at my brain and I became a prey to a rage of vengeance that had no sense and no purpose other than to strike at the man who seemed to be the destroyer of the Confederacy. I followed Candover's lead, I drew my friends into the plot, and you all know what followed.'

He fell silent again, and we were silent also for a while. Then Holmes said, 'And Candover betrayed you?'

'Yes,' said Booth. 'He betrayed me, but that is of the least account. Through me he betrayed my friends to the gallows – poor Mary Surratt who knew nothing of any assassination, who was only a part of the kidnap plan – she hanged through me and Candover. They might have hanged me – often I have wished that they had – but no, instead they let me live and hanged the others. Even poor Mudd, who did nothing, rotted for years in the Tortugas. And it was all to no purpose.'

'In what way?' I asked.

'The only purpose I had served was Candover's – his and his master's.'

'His master?' queried Holmes.

'Stanton!' hissed Booth. 'The Union's War Minister. He wanted Lincoln out of the way once the war was ended so that he and his kind could trample on the South and loot it and that is what they did. That is what I did. That is all I achieved for my country!'

The tears flowed freely down his yellowed cheeks and we gave him time to compose himself before Holmes spoke again.

120

'And was Tumbletye a part of this?'

'Tumbletye? No, whatever he is, he was not a traitor to the Confederacy. I met him in Canada. He was a Knight of the Golden Circle and he had managed to get himself attached to Maclellan's staff in Washington. He carried information and put forward plans. He was, I think, involved with Luke Blackburn in the plot to spread smallpox in the Union and maybe with the plan to burn New York. After Montreal I knew nothing of him until this year.'

'Where had you been?' asked Holmes.

'I told you the truth about that,' said Booth. 'I came first to England, like John Surratt. Then he went to Egypt and I went to India. I was in the Company's service, but you will not find the name Byron nor Booth in the Company's Green Books. My health was affected and it was then I came back to England. I had hoped to end my days here, but that is now impossible. I had even hoped that in the fullness of time, I might return, unnoticed, to America. Can you imagine, gentlemen, what it is to be a man with no nation, no identity, no home, bereft of friends and separated for ever from his wife? If Craig watches me, I dare not go home.'

'We cannot prevent Colonel Craig watching you,' said Holmes, 'but if you fear exposure at our hands you need not. Watson and I will not reveal your identity. Essex here already knew who you were and Colonel Craig would never permit him to reveal what he knows. However, in return for our silence you must tell us what you know of Tumbletye's plot against the Jubilee.'

'Another madman who believes that the world's wrongs can be righted by murder,' said Booth, and laughed harshly. 'You are right. He would have betrayed me for his own purposes, just as Candover did, and I should have died on a British rope instead of an American one.'

'Then what is his intention?' pressed Holmes.

'I do not know the details,' said Booth, 'but he intends to strike when Cody's show goes to Windsor Castle tomorrow. He says that there is a point in the performance when he can attack several of the royal guests at once. He means to commit such a slaughter of the Queen's guests that the Jubilee will become a day of mourning and national shame.'

121

'At what point will this occur?' asked Holmes.

Booth shook his head. 'I do not know,' he said. 'Tumbletye has said only that he has infiltrated men into Cody's show who will help him put down a royal flush, as he called it.'

'A royal flush,' mused Holmes. 'A hand of royal cards and an ace. What can he mean?'

'I do not know,' repeated Booth. 'Believe me, if I knew I would tell you. I have played the mad murderer once too often myself and I would not help him do the same.'

He struggled to his feet with the assistance of his long cane and wrapped his voluminous cape about himself.

'I do not believe that I can help you further, gentlemen,' he said and hobbled away.

'Is he really Booth?' I asked Holmes.

'Who else?' he demanded. 'Observe his lameness and recall that Dr Samuel Mudd was sentenced to the Dry Tortugas for his botched attempt to set Booth's broken ankle. All that he has told us fits and most of all it explains why Tumbletye has been so determined to involve Booth in his plot. With Tumbletye's insane grievance against the United States he would have left Booth to be blamed for whatever infamy occurred tomorrow and, thereby, branded the United States as liars before the world, liars even in the matter of the greatest crime ever committed on their soil.'

'What shall we do now?' I asked.

'We must see Cody,' said Holmes, decisively. 'We must ask him what part a royal flush may play in his entertainment, but first we must know Lestrade's answer. Come, Watson, there is little time.'

19

PROFESSIONAL COLLEAGUES

We returned to Baker Street where Holmes left the cab waiting and dashed upstairs. He returned with a telegram and thrust it wordlessly into my hand as he jumped back into the cab. It read:
LITTLECHILD ADAMANT STOP YOU MAY NOT ATTEND STOP LESTRADE.

'What had you requested?' I enquired.

'That you and I be permitted to join Lestrade's men at Windsor tomorrow,' he said. 'This is stupidity of an order unusual even at Scotland Yard!'

He ordered the cabbie to take us to the Yard and we rattled away. Holmes sat upright and drummed his long fingers impatiently upon his knee as we travelled.

At the Embankment he sprang out and was about to plunge into Scotland Yard's door when he paused.

'Mr Essex,' he said, 'I fear this is the point at which we must part company.'

Essex grinned. 'Come now, Mr Holmes. You know that I can't write this story and you know why. Surely you're not going to deprive me of the chance to be in at the kill. At least if you nail Tumbletye for plotting against your Queen, I can write that without Pericles Craig dropping on me.'

'It is not', said Holmes, 'that I fear what you may write, but I fear the way in which Chief Inspector Littlechild may react to you.'

'He dislikes reporters?' said Essex.

'He prefers his reporters to be tamed,' said Holmes. 'Those he feeds by hand with titbits of information which he has carefully prepared. You, alas, do not seem to be tame enough.'

Essex grinned again, ruefully. 'Then I guess you're right. This is the parting of the ways. Good luck, Mr Holmes,' and he touched his hat and sauntered away across the street.

123

'Mr Essex,' called Holmes and the American turned. 'Where might I find Colonel Cody?'

'He has chambers in Regent Street,' replied Essex. 'He's over the Hope Brothers shop, right next door to Blumenfeld of the *New York Herald*,' and he repeated his good wishes before turning away once more.

Holmes and I made our way inside where my friend demanded to be taken to Inspector Lestrade at once. We were led upstairs through warrens of small offices, until we reached the Detective Department, where Lestrade enjoyed the luxury of a tiny cubicle, barely big enough to contain a desk and chairs.

The detective looked startled as we entered. 'Mr Holmes, Doctor!' he exclaimed. 'What brings you here?'

'You know very well what brings us here,' snapped Holmes. 'Your fatuous telegram.'

The little policeman looked embarrassed. 'If it was me, Mr Holmes, I wouldn't have the least objection to your being at Windsor. No one can deny that your ideas, queer as they may be, have sometimes helped the Yard, and I freely admit that you've been helpful in the Tumbletye matter, but it's Mr Littlechild. He don't like private agents in general, and he's taken against you rather particularly, Mr Holmes. He says that you take fees from private persons and take all the credit when the Yard solves the case.'

No one had more frequently denied Sherlock Holmes' conclusions and then adopted them and claimed the public credit than the man who sat before us, but he did, at the least have the grace not to look my friend in the eye during this recitation.

Holmes was unruffled. 'Then take me to Littlechild,' he demanded. 'I have further information – urgent information!'

Lestrade looked out of the window. 'It's very difficult, Mr Holmes. The Chief Inspector's a busy man at present. You've always felt able to share your confidences with me in the past,' he went on, 'why not let me hear your new information and then I can act upon it?'

'My information', said Holmes, 'is incomplete, but I have confirmed that Tumbletye's attempt will be made at Windsor tomorrow.'

'Then we can take especial care to protect Her Majesty,' said Lestrade.

'It is not the Queen who will be the centre of Tumbletye's plot,' said Holmes, 'and I do not know who will be. It is essential that Watson and I are there.'

Lestrade shook his head. 'I can't do it, Mr Holmes. I daren't risk it. If you was to get into the Queen's party tomorrow, Mr Littlechild would break me down to constable or even throw me off the Force, I dare say. I can't do it.'

'Then take me to Littlechild,' Holmes demanded again.

An expression of resignation passed across Lestrade's sallow features and he pressed a button on his desk. A constable knocked and entered.

'Constable,' said Lestrade, 'take these gentlemen to Mr Little-child, and Mr Holmes – I hope you'll be at pains to point out that I have made no agreements with you, merely passed on my orders from Mr Littlechild.'

'Oh, indeed,' said Holmes, tersely.

We set out upon another journey through corridors until our guide brought us to a waiting-room equipped only with upright chairs. Bidding us take seats the constable tapped a door and announced to someone within that Inspector Lestrade had sent two visitors along. He withdrew to tell us that we must wait, then left.

We waited – how long I do not know. It may have been as much as an hour that we sat in that dusty waiting-room, listening to the mournful hoots of tugboats on the river and the footsteps of policemen and clerks scurrying along the corridors outside. Holmes sat rigidly, his face a mask and his fingers drumming interminably upon his knee. After our uncomfortable night and our strenuous escape from Tumbletye's clutches, I had difficulty in remaining awake.

At last the inner door opened and a man in civilian clothes appeared. 'Mr Littlechild will see you now,' he told us and we followed him into the Chief Inspector's office.

Littlechild sat with his back to a window that overlooked the Embankment and the Thames, at a desk littered with papers. He was a large man, with protuberant eyes and a large moustache, similar in appearance to the late Lord Kitchener. He looked up as we entered and nodded us silently to two empty chairs in front of the desk.

'I am Sherlock Holmes – ' began my friend, once we were seated, but Littlechild interrupted him.

Jerking his chin up, so as to expose his muscular neck, he said, 'I know who you are. You're the private agent. What d'you want with me?'

'You will be aware that I have given Inspector Lestrade certain information regarding the man Tumbletye,' said Holmes.

'Yes,' said Littlechild. 'What of it?'

'I understand that Lestrade has put to you my request that Dr Watson and I should be permitted to join your officers at the performance of the Wild West Show at Windsor tomorrow,' said Holmes.

'Indeed,' said Littlechild. 'I imagine that you are, by now, aware that I have refused to allow it.'

'May I ask why?' enquired Holmes.

'Why?' snapped the detective. 'Why? Because it's preposterous, that's why!' He gestured at his cluttered desk. 'Mr Williamson is away and I have in my hands the planning and execution of all the arrangements for tomorrow's entertainment at Windsor and the whole of the Jubilee celebration the day after, and one of my officers comes to me with a request that I should allow two private citizens to mingle with the official police at Windsor tomorrow. The idea is ludicrous – the entire intention of my arrangements is to limit the number and nature of persons at Windsor apart from Her Majesty's family and her guests.'

Holmes' mouth was a thin line but his voice was even. 'I am able', he said, 'to confirm that Tumbletye's attack will occur at Windsor, but it will not be directed at Her Majesty.'

'And how do you know that?' demanded Littlechild.

'Because Tumbletye himself has told me so,' said Holmes.

'And you take the word of that madman?' scoffed the Chief Inspector. 'Has it not occurred to you, Mr Holmes, that he has done it to mislead you – and through you, me?'

'Your officers have not, in the past, found reason to doubt the veracity of my information,' said Holmes.

'And very useful it has been!' exclaimed Littlechild. 'Lestrade sought my advice when he learned that you had come across

126

Tumbletye in your enquiries, and I advised him to let you carry on and see what information you could supply. What has that led to? The accidental arrest of two of Tumbletye's henchmen – if they are indeed his men – who you say have perpetrated at least two murders but against whom we have no evidence of anything worse than being equipped for burglary. I do not regard that as a significant contribution to Scotland Yard's attempts to protect the Queen, Mr Holmes.'

Holmes drew a long breath. 'Mr Littlechild,' he said, 'my reason for wishing to be present tomorrow is a simple one. I am aware that Tumbletye proposes not to attack the Queen but to inflict some outrage that will gravely embarrass Her Majesty and the Empire. I am also aware that he has used the expression "royal flush" in reference to what he proposes.'

'And what', demanded Littlechild, 'does that mean?'

'At present I do not know,' replied Holmes. 'It may be that I can discover the meaning before tomorrow, in which case I shall certainly inform Inspector Lestrade, but if I cannot, then it would be a great deal safer for the Queen's guests if Watson and I are permitted to attend.'

'And what is the source of your information?'

'I cannot reveal that,' said Holmes. 'You may take it that I am sufficiently satisfied that my informant was genuinely in Tumbletye's confidence.'

'Oh I may, may I?' jeered Littlechild. 'You appear to be talking about a fellow conspirator of Tumbletye's, Holmes – another damned Fenian. If I wished I could have you arrested for attempting to pervert the course of justice. However, I am far too busy to waste any more time on your theories. Numbers of my officers have expressed the view that your approach to detection is fanciful and theoretical and that, when you do achieve results, it is largely by good luck. I have to say that, in this matter, your luck has run out. Good afternoon, gentlemen.'

Holmes rose and stalked out of the room without a word, his face as pale as marble.

Outside Scotland Yard he hailed a cab and asked to be taken to Regent Street.

20

AN AMERICAN ALLY

I had, of course, read much of the exploits of Colonel Cody and I already regarded him as one of the most extraordinary men of this or any other age. Even discounting the exaggerations of journalists, this was a man who, at the age of only eleven years, had shot down an Indian creeping up on the wagon train for which Bill Cody was a messenger, at fourteen had ridden for the Pony Express, and had gone on to scout for the Union through the Civil War, battle with Indians hand-to-hand and exercise his remarkable marksmanship on the great buffalo herds of the western plains. I was, therefore, prepared for an exceptional individual, but I still recall the astonishment with which I viewed the great showman as he rose from his chair by the window of his chambers.

He was then a little beyond fifty, an age at which most successful men begin to let the pace slacken, but Cody moved with the vigour of a man thirty years younger and projected a vibrant energy. His handsome locks framed his face like those of a young Cavalier, his beard and moustaches curled crisply, and his eyes were bright and steady.

I had also been prepared for the excesses of costume for which Americans are well known. Cody was dressed in a white satin shirt, cut buccaneer-style, with a red handkerchief at his throat. His dark red trousers were flared at the bottoms like a sailor's and trimmed at the sides with silver adornments while his feet were encased in richly decorated moccasins.

He rose with a bright smile lighting his handsome features and clasped Holmes' hand in both of his.

'Why, Sherlock!' he exclaimed. 'Ever since we docked I've been trying to make the time to see you and here you are!' He indicated the clusters of flowers that filled one side of the room.

'You mustn't mind those,' he said, 'the ladies of London will keep sending them, fresh every day.'

He scrutinised my friend closely. 'It has been a darned long time, Sherlock, but you seem to have done well on it. When I got to London and asked about you, they told me you were the most famous detective in all England.'

Holmes smiled warmly. 'It is remarkably good to see you again, Colonel. Dr Watson and I have been reading the accounts of your success at Kensington and planning to come and see your display, but work has intervened and I regret to say that it is work that now brings us here.'

'No matter, no matter,' said Cody, and ushered us to chairs.

'Now,' he said, once we were seated and he had thrust cigars and tumblers of American whisky upon us, 'what work brings you here, my friend?'

Holmes outlined his enquiries to the American. When Tumbletye's name was first mentioned the Colonel exclaimed and slapped his thigh.

'Tumbletye!' he said. 'That snake! He's here in London?'

'You know him?' said Holmes.

'I surely do,' said Cody. 'I have run across him maybe a dozen times back home. He even had the nerve to suggest that he should be in my show.'

'What do you know of him?' enquired Holmes.

'That he's crazy as a loon and poisonous as a rattlesnake, Sherlock. He worked both sides during the war and I've heard tell he was a friend of Booth who shot the President. They took him up for being mixed up in that, but they let him go. They ought to have hanged him with the others. What's his business in London?'

Holmes continued his narrative of our enquiries though concealing the identity of poor Booth. When he had done he struck off a number of points on his fingers.

'So you see,' he told the Colonel, 'we know that he will strike tomorrow, we know that he is not intending direct harm to the Queen and we know that what he intends is designed to embarrass both Britain and the United States. That must mean that the scene of his attack will be Windsor while your show is there.'

129

Cody nodded thoughtfully. 'All you don't know', he reflected, 'is just what it is that he's up to. It's a humdinger, ain't it?'

'It is indeed', said my friend, 'a humdinger.'

'Half the crowned heads of Europe will be there,' said the Colonel. 'He might do anything – a bomb, rifle fire – who knows what?'

'Who is to be present?' asked Holmes.

The American picked up a newspaper from a side table and scanned it.

'It says here that the King of Greece will be there with Prince George, and the King of Saxony, the King and Queen of Belgium, the King of Denmark, the Austrian Crown Prince, the Prince and Princess of Saxe-Meininger, the Norwegian Crown Prince, the Princess Victoria of Prussia, the Duke of Sparta, the Grand Duke Michael of Russia, Prince Louis of Baden. Then, of course, apart from your Queen, the Prince and Princess of Wales will be there.'

'Great heavens!' I exclaimed. 'If Tumbletye were to achieve any serious attack on that company while your show is in progress, Colonel, it would damage relations between Britain, the United States and most of Europe!'

'Precisely,' said Holmes. 'He has chosen his time and place well. Tell me, Colonel, what exactly will take place at Windsor? How will your entertainment be presented?'

'Well,' said Cody, 'Nate Salisbury and I have been down to the Castle and looked over the ground. There's going to be a big tent with one side open set up on what they call the East Terrace. That'll be for the comfort of Her Majesty and all them fancy guests. The seats and the food and drink will be there. We shall perform on the lawns below the terrace in the open.'

Holmes nodded. 'And what, exactly, constitutes your show?'

'It's kind of difficult to put it shortly, unless you say it's mainly displays of riding and shooting.'

He reached to the side table and passed both of us copies of a programme pamphlet. It showed that, apart from cowboys and Red Indians, the show's cast included Mexicans, Cossacks, Gauchos, Arabs and detachments of the American, British, German and Russian armies. I could see at a glance that there were numerous items included in the performance that might provide cover for an attack on the royal party by bomb or gun.

130

'The display of artillery drill by the American army', said Holmes, 'presumably includes the firing of shells?'

'Surely,' said Cody. 'You can't show folks how a gun is set up in battle and then not let them hear the bang. But they're blanks, Sherlock.'

'Let us hope so,' said Holmes, and returned to his perusal of the programme.

A moment later he asked, 'And are blanks used in the "Attack on an Emigrant Train", the "Attack on Settlers' Cabins" and the "Attack on the Deadwood Mailcoach"?'

'Of course,' said the Colonel. 'There's a great deal of gunplay in those items. You can't guarantee that a stray shot won't go astray and injure someone in the audience. 'Twouldn't do at all to go killing or maiming the customers.'

Holmes looked thoughtful. 'But the displays of marksmanship by yourself, Mr Baker and Miss Oakley will, I imagine, involve the use of live rounds.'

Cody nodded. 'Yes,' he said. 'That's target shooting at glass balls thrown in the air and that kind of thing. Can't be faked, you've got to hit the target.'

'I confess', said Holmes, 'that I like this situation less and less. Here we have a company of – how many, Colonel?'

'About five hundred performers and a few hundred others,' said Cody.

'A company of several hundred people of all nationalities in a wide variety of costumes, the discharge of artillery, numbers of people dashing about firing rifles and pistols – I do not like it one little bit, Colonel.'

'I am told there will be a party of Scotland Yard officers present,' said Cody.

'So am I,' said Holmes, grimly. 'But like us, they will not know what they are looking for.'

'Will you be there?' asked the Colonel.

'I', said my friend, 'have been expressly forbidden to involve myself by Mr Littlechild at Scotland Yard.'

'I thought he was a stuffed shirt,' said Cody, 'but I didn't realise he was a fool as well. If that's the case, you and the Doctor will have to come with us.'

'With you?' queried Holmes, as though the idea had never crossed his mind.

'Why not?' demanded the American. 'There are hundreds of us going down by a special train in the morning.'

He looked us over with narrowed eyes. 'Of course,' he said, 'neither of you looks much like any of my crowd at the moment, but I seem to recall you're pretty smart at looking like who you ain't, Sherlock.'

Holmes smiled. 'I'm sure we can manage to blend in with your men,' he said.

'Then that's settled,' said Cody. 'You and Dr Watson will come down as part of my crew. I shall feel a darn sight happier if I know you're in the column, Sherlock.'

Holmes drummed his fingers. 'I should feel a great deal happier if we had some indication of when Tumbletye will strike.'

'We'll all just have to keep our eyes peeled,' said Cody.

Holmes was silent for a moment, then he picked up the programme again. 'Tell me,' he said, 'are any of the displays in here known as a "royal flush"?'

Cody's jaw dropped. 'How in tarnation did you come to hear that?' he demanded. 'That was a joke of mine.'

'A joke?' queried Holmes.

'Yep. When Nate and I and Major Burke were down at Windsor the other day, the Prince of Wales was there. Now it ain't the first time we've met and he's a regular guy. We got to talking about which pieces of the show we'd be doing tomorrow, and of course he wanted the big spectacular bits – the wagon train and the cabin attack and the Deadwood Stage. I told him I was leaving all those in and he said that he and some of his crowd wanted to ride in the Deadwood Stage for the attack. Now, who did he say it was...?'

Cody paused and his brow creased while he thought. Then he snapped his fingers.

'I have it!' he exclaimed. 'Prince Edward said that he and the King of Greece, the King of Norway, the King of Denmark and the King of Belgium wanted to ride the Deadwood Stage. I said of course they could and I made a joke. I said something like, "Four kings and an ace? That'll be the finest royal flush in history,'' and he laughed. That's all it was, Sherlock, a joke. How come you heard about it?'

Holmes was grinning broadly. 'Tumbletye boasted about his plan to a contact, saying something about a royal flush. He has given himself away, Colonel. The attack will be on the stage-coach.'

'It's a good way to do it,' said Cody. 'It wouldn't take much to get himself four kings and the heir to the throne of England.'

'What takes place in that part of the programme?' asked Holmes.

'Well, Johnny Burke drives the coach, same as he used to when it was on the road up in Dakota. He does a bit of fancy driving, then a war party of redskins comes on and attacks the coach and then I come on with a party of cowboys and we see the Indians off and rescue the coach and passengers.'

'And your redskins?' said Holmes. 'Are they all from America?'

'They all came over with me,' said the Colonel. 'Most of them have been with us for a long time.' He grinned. 'I don't think you need to worry about them – I don't guess we've got any Fenian redskins or Confederate redskins!'

'True,' acknowledged Holmes, 'though an attack by the red men would have been the ideal means for Tumbletye, since that is what everyone expects them to do. What about your cowboys? Have they all come with you?'

'Well, no,' said Cody. 'All we need of most of them is to ride well and shoot blanks, so when we're short-handed we can usually find Americans locally to fill the gaps.'

'You have taken on men in London?' asked Holmes.

'Some two or three,' said Cody. 'Do you want me to pull them out of the show?'

'Certainly not,' said Holmes. 'If we do not permit Tumbletye's attempt at Windsor, he will try somewhere else where we are not ready for him. He may attack the procession on Jubilee Day or who knows what. No, we must let his plan go ahead and defeat it.'

'Are you not taking rather a risk with the safety of the Prince of Wales and his friends?' I ventured.

133

'I do not believe so,' said Holmes. 'Better this way, with you and me and the Colonel knowing exactly what is going on, than to leave them exposed to chance attack later.'

The Colonel gave us details of his special train in the morning and we left.

'Come, Watson,' said Holmes, cheerfully. 'We must spend a little time in making you look like an American.'

I was always cheered by the prospect of action, but I admit that I had mixed feelings about going into action disguised as an American.

21

AMERICANS AT WINDSOR

My misgivings were not allayed when we returned to Baker Street. No sooner had we taken our dinner than Holmes began to eye me narrowly across the table.

'Is there something strange about me?' I asked him, at length.

'No, no,' he said. 'That may be the problem. There is nothing the least bit strange about you, Watson.'

I bridled a little, not liking the implications of his remark, but he went on.

'Please do not take offence, my dear fellow. I was merely considering our task tomorrow and the necessity of appearing as two members of Cody's show. Now I, as you have been good enough to admit, have no little experience and ability when it comes to passing myself off in disguise, but a single glance at you will reveal you to be an Englishman of the professional classes and most probably a bachelor. We must consider how we can make you a little more flamboyant, Watson.'

'I am not at all sure', I said, 'that I wish to be made flamboyant.'

'It is not, alas, a question of our wishes, Watson. Tomorrow we must pass for some hours as unnoticeable members of a troupe which includes cowboys, redskins, Cossacks, Arabs – almost every manner of man except a plain ordinary Englishman such as yourself.'

He drew on his pipe and a thoughtful expression appeared on his face.

'Did you not', he said, after a moment or two, 'purchase a rather strange, yellowish suit last summer, Watson?'

'I recall a light brown summer suit which seemed to arouse your sense of humour,' I replied.

'No doubt that is the one,' he said. 'If we were not so disparate in build I could readily supply you from my own array of costumes, but as things are we shall have to build upon your own duds and, perhaps, add a few properties that will increase the verisimilitude of the deception. I wonder if you would be good enough to fetch it out when you have finished your smoke?'

In the privacy of my room I examined the garments in question. I had not worn the suit since the previous summer because, if truth is to be told, I had come to share Holmes' perceptions of it. The light brown was a degree too orangey and the check a point or so too loud. I shuddered inwardly at the thought of appearing before Her Majesty in such a suit adorned with whatever Holmes meant when he spoke of 'properties'.

It occurred to me that a soft-collared shirt might be appropriate so I changed into one, put on the suit and returned to the sitting-room.

Holmes lifted the lamp from the table and examined me thoroughly.

'Capital! Capital, Watson!' he exclaimed. 'We shall make an actor of you yet. The soft collar is exactly right, though it needs something dramatic in the way of ties to look properly American and I suggest a hat of a somewhat overlarge variety.'

He disappeared towards his room and returned in minutes, with a selection of hats and ties. After trying several, each more ludicrous than its predecessor, he settled on a flowing tie with wide white spots on a plum background, then turned his attention to headgear. I rejected absolutely a purplish billycock which seemed to appeal to him.

'A shame,' he remarked as he cast it aside. 'It was with that hat that I supported the character of Cholsker the Danish clown when I tracked Grogan the one-legged strongman to his lair.'

In the end I accepted a wide-brimmed, low-crowned grey hat which, if it had not been married to the suit and tie, might have been quite wearable.

Holmes gazed thoughtfully at my feet. 'Footgear,' he said. 'So many excellent disguises are ruined by inappropriate footgear. Remind me to tell you someday how I unmasked the Spanish assassin Garedor because he wore the wrong shoes.'

'I refuse', I said, 'to wear pointed boots with high heels, and certainly not those preposterous jingle devices that Cody's cowboys wear!'

'That will not, I think, be required,' he said. 'A robust pair of brown shoes should be sufficient.'

When they had been found and put on I was subjected to a final inspection. Holmes walked around me as though I were an exhibit in Madame Tussaud's before expressing himself satisfied.

'It is very convincing, Watson, but I fear the effect will be spoiled if you smoke a pipe or cigarettes. Cigars are, I think, the thing. There is also the question of your speech. I have at my disposal a range of the regional accents of the United States, but I do not think there is time to tutor you. Perhaps you had better let me do the talking or, if pressed, adopt a monosyllabic style. You had best carry a sheaf of papers and appear to be making notes – people will take you to be some kind of official and steer clear of you.'

I was about to return to my room and change my clothes when he remarked over his shoulder, 'By the way, Watson – keep the hands in the trouser pockets when possible and slouch more.'

We retired early, and I did not have the privilege of seeing Holmes' costume until I arrived at the breakfast table, where I found myself seated opposite the Reverend Hiram McCandless. A strip of ragged black beard fringed Holmes' face, small spectacles bridged his nose and his long form was clad in a shabby black frock coat, waistcoat and trousers. At his neck a high collar was decorated with a straggling narrow tie whose bow escaped in all directions. When we rose to leave he added a wide-brimmed straw hat and a small Bible to his ensemble.

At the siding where Cody's train was being assembled all was apparent confusion as men, women, animals, vehicles, props and scenery arrived and were loaded. Gradually, however, order prevailed and the train was loaded.

We were taken to the Colonel's carriage, where he greeted us warmly, and the short journey to Windsor was almost entirely taken up with his jokes at our appearance. At our destination I began to perceive that there was, in fact, a very great orderliness in the apparent confusion of Cody's cast and helpers; that each section was under the firm command of one person who knew exactly what he required. In an astonishingly short time the train

137

had been emptied, its contents transferred to the lawn of the Castle and the Wild West Show was ready to commence.

As the Cowboy Band opened the proceedings with 'The Star-Spangled Banner', Holmes and I stood with Cody behind the screens that concealed the 'off-stage' area from the royal audience.

'There are three of them,' said the Colonel, in answer to a question from Holmes. 'They have all been taken on since we came to London and they are all due to ride with me in the rescue of the Deadwood coach.'

'Then we are right,' said Holmes. 'That is Tumbletye's target.'

I was still uneasy at the idea that the plot should be allowed to go ahead.

'Surely,' I said, 'if Colonel Cody were to change the arrangements so that those three men were not involved with the coach it would be a great deal safer for the royal party?'

'For today maybe,' said Holmes, 'but Tumbletye would then strike elsewhere at another time, as I said yesterday. No, Watson, the plot must be allowed to run and we must ensure that no harm comes to Her Majesty's guests.'

'Doc,' said the Colonel, 'this Tumbletye character has chosen my show to serve his purposes and I ain't having it. If he got away with it, England'll blame America because it's my show, America'll blame England for letting it happen and all Europe'll blame both of us. So it's up to us to stop it, and the best place to do that is here. Tumbletye's picked the pitch – now let's play him on his chosen ground.'

He walked off and Holmes, seeing that I remained doubtful, remarked, 'The Prince of Wales and his guests have been warned that there will be a great deal of gunplay when the rescue is staged and that no one can guarantee that there won't be wads from blank ammunition flying about. He has been requested to ask his guests to keep back from the coach windows once the cowboys appear.'

The overture ended and Colonel Cody led out the Grand Review procession to loud applause from the watchers on the terrace. Backstage, Holmes seemed entirely unruffled, calmly watching the performance through a slit in the canvas screen. If anyone drew near he would smile broadly at them and try to engage them in religious conversation. His theory worked inasmuch as they broke off the conversation and withdrew as rapidly as possible, having no opportunity to discover whether I could speak American or not.

I, too, found a convenient eyehole in the screens and began to enjoy the show. I was rapt with wonder at Miss Annie Oakley, the petite, long-haired lass whose artistry with a rifle was magical.

'Have you ever seen the like of that?' I demanded of Holmes.

'No,' he replied, 'nor have we seen a sight of Lestrade or any of his men, despite the fact that an expert rifle shot, using live ammunition, is out there on the lawn, a few feet from Her Majesty and her guests!'

'But Holmes!' I protested. 'That is Miss Oakley! The Queen has met her personally. There cannot be any danger.'

'The possibility of danger exists,' he insisted, 'and Lestrade should have taken precautions.'

The splendid performance flowed on, each act seemingly more astounding, more daring, more skilful than the last and each earning gales of applause from the royal party. Cossacks, Mexicans, Arabs, soldiers of several nations, cowboys, redskins and Pony Express riders demonstrated their skills with horses and their speed and daring in the saddle; cowboys showed their abilities to handle cattle with a whirling rope, redskins danced and drummed, soldiers exhibited their equestrian drills, military bands played, guns were fired endlessly, some loaded with blanks, some with live ammunition.

I had almost forgotten the reasons why we were there and become totally absorbed in the spectacle passing before our eyes, when Cody himself rode out to demonstrate his marksmanship. Near to us, as the Colonel performed, the Deadwood Stagecoach was being prepared and its team harnessed. A strange figure in uniform trousers and long boots, with his wide braces over a dark blue shirt, appeared and sauntered towards Holmes and me. Under a battered, wide-brimmed felt hat the stranger's weathered features peered through an enormous burst of grey beard.

'Howdy!' he greeted us. 'You must be Sherlock Holmes and Doc Watson?'

I made no reply, shocked that this man seemed to have penetrated our disguise, but Holmes held out his hand.

'You', he said, 'must be Mr Burke?'

'Johnny Burke,' the stranger replied, shaking hands warmly with both of us. 'I drive the stage.'

'Colonel Cody has told you what is afoot?' asked Holmes.

'Surely,' said Burke, 'and I guess it'll make things a bit more realistic. Be the first time the old coach has been really attacked for a good few years.'

'The situation doesn't worry you?' I asked.

'If I worried easy,' he said, 'I'd never have driven a stage in the first place. What with bad roads and ornery passengers, road agents and redskins, it ain't the easiest way to make a living.'

Holmes chuckled. 'You know what we plan to do?' he asked.

'Yup, I think so. You two will ride on top. We go out, I do a big wide pass with the coach, we pull up by the tent so as the Prince and his pals can get inside. Once we're loaded, I start a long figure of eight and, while we're doing it, the redskins come whoopin' at us. I drive up and down a piece while they make a lot of noise and shoot a parcel of arrows around us. When Colonel Cody thinks that has gone on long enough, he comes out with the cowboys and chases after the redskins.'

'That', said Holmes, 'is where it becomes dangerous. You know that three of the cowboys may be intent on murdering the coach's passengers?'

'Sure I do,' said Burke, 'but there's the Colonel and me, and you two on top, to stop 'em. The Colonel says it's them three over there,' and he jerked a thumb over his shoulder.

A group of cowboys loitered, watching the coach being prepared, but there were six or so and I saw no great difference in any of them.

'Which three?' asked Holmes.

'White hats and green bandannas,' said Burke. 'You'll spot 'em easy enough.'

'White hats and green neckerchiefs,' said Holmes. 'Remember that, Watson.'

A round of applause sounded from beyond the screens.

140

'Looks like the Colonel's done,' said Burke. 'We're next, gentlemen. All aboard as is coming aboard.'

He clambered up to his seat on the coach's front and Holmes and I scrambled to positions on the roof. Burke emitted a piercing yell and cracked his long whip and the Deadwood Stage moved off.

22

A ROYAL PERFORMANCE

When I was a boy the coach had not disappeared from English roads; it was still fulfilling a useful role in carrying goods and passengers in areas not reached by the railway. As a result I was well used to 'riding outside' as we called it, perched up on the roof of a coach rattling through the back roads.

However, I was alarmed on reaching the roof of the Deadwood coach to find that there were no passenger seats, only an expanse of railed roof at the rear of which a quantity of dummy luggage had been strapped.

'Holmes!' I exclaimed. 'How shall we keep our position?'

'I suggest you hold on to the rail, Watson. At least we have the advantage of a view all around.'

I sat with my back to Mr Burke's driving-seat and grasped the roof rail firmly as we swung out on to the lawn. As Burke had said, he made a sweeping pass across the area, then swung the vehicle in so tight an arc as nearly to dislodge me from my perch. As I regained my hand-hold we slowed and halted in front of the royal party's tent.

Prince Edward stepped out, swung open the door of the coach and showed his four guests inside, before jumping inside and taking his seat. The door slammed and the Prince called, 'Take her away, Mr Burke!'

We pulled away and soon Burke had the coach jogging steadily across a wide arc of the lawn. Then came the chilling ululation of redskin war-cries, and a party of braves mounted on ponies burst around the screens and came after us.

Our driver seemed to be whipping up his horses, though in reality he was skilfully keeping the action within the frame of the lawn, as the first of the braves began to catch up with us. A shower of blunted arrows hurtled over our heads, and Holmes and I sprawled flat on the coach's roof.

The coach swung again in a tight turn, scattering the nearest Indians, but soon they were alongside us once more and another shower of arrows burst over us while they kept up their frightening yells.

Then a single pistol shot sounded. Holmes said, 'Now be ready, Watson!' and drew a pistol from his pocket. I took out my Adams .450 and looked around. Behind us, Cody and half a dozen cowboys were riding down upon the Indians, brandishing rifles and pistols. We could clearly distinguish Tumbletye's men in the group.

'Do not give them a chance, Watson!' yelled Holmes. 'If one of them points a weapon in this direction, shoot him!'

Some of the redskins had drawn rifles from scabbards on their ponies, and the early stages of the battle were an exchange of rifle-fire at a little distance. The three conspirators had held themselves to the rear of Cody's band, presumably so that it would be difficult for an observer to see whether they were firing at the Indians or at the coach. Now one of them came down behind the Indian party, seemingly seeking to get closer to the window of the stagecoach. As he lifted his rifle, I gripped the roof rail firmly, levelled my Adams as well as I might, and fired.

His rifle spun into the air as my shot went home, and a moment later he dropped from his saddle. One of his fellows swung to look as he fell, then pulled his horse up short and scanned the coach narrowly. I realised that we had lost the advantage of surprise, for he now knew that live rounds were being fired from the coach.

Holmes had his eye on another of the three, who was attempting to repeat his dead colleague's manoeuvre, positioning himself so that an apparent shot at the Indians could be fired into the coach. It was a few moments before he found the right position and when he did, a redskin arrow skimmed so close to him that he drew up and fell behind the action.

The coach came round in another of Burke's dramatic turns, and Tumbletye's men were both now in wrong positions, but it was only seconds before one of them found a new vantage. It was the one who had watched his comrade fall and when he lifted his rifle it was to fire at us, not at the coach's window.

Three shots ripped across the roof, closer than I cared to experience. I found that I could not keep as close to the surface of the roof as I might have wished and have a reasonable view of the action. I decided to take the risk and sat up.

'Get down, Watson!' called Holmes, but I launched myself in a spring that took me to the stack of luggage at the rear of the roof and slid behind it as another three bullets whistled past.

I could now brace myself better by clinging to the luggage straps and had better cover against fire from the ground. Peering cautiously around the pile of trunks I spotted a green bandanna and laid a bead on its wearer. He lifted his rifle and two shots rang out, as Holmes and I took him simultaneously.

I watched him pitch from his horse and sprawl motionless then cast my eyes around to find the third white hat. At first I could not see it, but then I caught glimpses of it, flashes as its wearer passed rapidly behind both the Indian band and Cody's cowboys. Evidently he understood the danger from Holmes and me and intended to keep as much cover as possible between himself and the coach.

I kept my pistol trained on him as closely as I might, but his position meant that I could never be sure of hitting him, rather than an Indian rider or one of the genuine cowboys.

I had grown used to the length of the arcs in which Johnny Burke swung the coach, and less disturbed by the turns, but as the next swing approached I was astounded to see Holmes rise to a crouch. As Burke turned the coach, Holmes suddenly stood and then launched himself over the roof rail.

I could not stop watching the white-hatted assassin weaving behind the redskins, but I was desperately anxious for Holmes and grateful when, after seconds, I saw him on the back of an Indian pony racing up behind the Indians.

He plunged in among the Indians, ostensibly to do battle with them, but he never plied his pistol. Then Tumbletye's third man passed alongside the Indians again, lifting his rifle to take advantage of a gap that would have given him a clear shot at the occupants of the coach. Holmes' revolver puffed smoke and the man fell.

My friend extracted himself from among the Indians and made his way to Colonel Cody's side. Cody called something

144

out and the Indians raced away while Burke slowed the coach and brought it to a halt.

I slid down from the coach on to a very realistic depiction of the aftermath of battle. Redskins, playing dead or injured, lay around, not to mention the three cowboys, and a haze of gunsmoke drifted in the sunshine.

Cody approached the Deadwood coach, tipped his big hat to the occupants and waved a hand to Johnny Burke. The coach swung slowly back to the front of the terrace, where its passengers disembarked in high good humour as a storm of applause greeted them and acknowledged the actors in the drama. I wondered what Her Majesty's guests might have thought had they known the truth of the dramatic display that had been played out in front of them.

Holmes, in his clerical guise, had examined the three cowboys where they lay and now approached me to tell me that one was still alive. 'They will be taken backstage in the coach,' he said. 'If you will look at him, we may save him as a witness against Tumbletye.'

Behind the canvas screens I examined all three. Two were plainly dead, but the third, though shot through the chest, still lived. With the assistance of Cody's medical men I patched him up and believed that there was no reason why he should not recover.

Once the last act of the show was over and Cody had ridden before Her Majesty with the Union flag and the Stars and Stripes, the applause was long and loud. The cheers were still ringing across the lawn when Cody, clad now in one of his resplendent white outfits, fringed and spangled, came to us.

'Well, Sherlock,' he said, smiling broadly, 'we did it. We saved the royal flush, we saved our two countries from embarrassment and it's mostly due to you.'

'You do me too much honour, Colonel,' said Holmes. 'I have merely pursued an enquiry along a logical path. Now I must pursue it to its end.'

'But Tumbletye's plan is frustrated!' I exclaimed. 'What more is there?'

' "We have scotched the snake, not killed it",' he quoted. 'Tumbletye is still at large and in Britain. If he does not know already, he will soon know that this attempt has failed. He may then try elsewhere. To prevent that, we must find him and arrest him.'

He turned to Cody. 'Colonel,' he said, 'I am deeply grateful to you for your wholehearted assistance in this matter. May I ask one more favour of you?'

'Ask away,' said Cody.

'Will you find Inspector Lestrade, who by now may well be in the vicinity of the buffet, and acquaint him with what has passed here. Ask him, also, to wire the ports to watch for Tumbletye. He may cut his losses and run for the Continent.'

'Surely,' said the great scout, and lifting a hand to his hat in farewell he strode away. Holmes and I were to see him once more when, the Jubilee over, we finally fulfilled our intention of visiting the show at Kensington and enjoying it in rather more comfortable circumstances than we had at Windsor. On that night we dined with Cody and I heard from his lips some of the greatest adventure tales of our time in which he had played a leading part. It is little more than a year since his death, by which the world has lost a true hero and a great gentleman. When I recall him it is always on that afternoon at Windsor, tipping the brim of his great white hat and stepping jauntily away, resplendent in white and silver.

In minutes Holmes and I were at the Castle gate where, to my surprise, we were met by Wiggins, leader of the Irregulars.

'He's packed up, Mr Holmes,' said the boy. 'We watched his gaff, like you said, and he packed his trunks and come down here in his four-wheeler.'

'So how did you get here?' demanded Holmes.

'On the back of his four-wheeler, didn't I?' he grinned.

'What did he do when he got here?' asked Holmes.

'He just sat in his carriage, near the Castle here. Then about a quarter of an hour ago he upped and went.'

'Which way?' asked Holmes.

The boy pointed. Holmes rubbed his chin. 'Then he was not going back to London. What is he up to, I wonder?'

He gazed silently down the road indicated by Wiggins for a few seconds.

'What shall we do?' I ventured.

'Do?' he said. 'Why, follow him, of course! We must know what he is about or all of today's efforts will be useless. We must acquire transport.'

I looked round me, in search of a cab, but saw none. At that moment I heard a cheerful voice hailing me.

'Why, Watson!' it called. 'Been calling on the Queen in fancy dress? What are you doing here?'

23

HOT PURSUIT

The excitement of events at the Castle had driven from my mind any consideration of the peculiar costumes which Holmes and I wore, but being hailed by name in a public street brought back to me forcibly an awareness of my appearance.

I looked quickly about me and saw that the cry had come from across the street, where Arthur Binstead, Newnham-Davis and Essex were emerging from the door of a public house. They were all in summer flannels and straw hats, though even that casual dress did not seem to lessen Binstead's formality or reduce his misleading appearance of gravity.

They swarmed across the street with cries of delight at recognising me. Essex stood back, grinning at my discomfiture and obviously aware of how Holmes and I came to be where we were.

'You'll never get into the Castle dressed like that,' said the Dwarf. 'Besides, it's "invitation only" today. We tried to get in as members of the press, but they weren't having it.'

'I have been assisting Holmes with an enquiry at the Castle,' I said, profoundly embarrassed. 'A degree of disguise was necessary. What are you all doing here?' I asked, in an attempt to divert attention from myself.

'We', said Binstead, 'have considered that our journalistic duties will be long and arduous at tomorrow's festivities. Hence we decided to hire a carriage and come for a relaxing trip on the river in preparation.'

'A carriage?' interrupted Holmes who had taken no notice at all of my friends up to that point. 'Did you say that you have a carriage, Binstead?'

'A very fine equipage,' said Binstead, 'seats for six and two very fine bays. Can we give you and Watson a lift anywhere?'

'It is not a lift that we require,' said Holmes. 'At this very moment a man who has today attempted to take the lives of the Prince of Wales and four of Her Majesty's guests is escaping along that road. I fear we need to commandeer your vehicle.'

'A pursuit!' exclaimed Newnham-Davis. 'Ripping! Essex, fetch the carriage. Mr Holmes' needs are greater than ours.'

Essex sprang away immediately, and Binstead addressed Holmes.

'Our vehicle is entirely at your command, Mr Holmes, but upon one condition – we must accompany you and Watson on this pursuit.'

'The man may be armed,' said Holmes. 'And he may have confederates. Watson and I have pistols but – '

Binstead raised his cane. 'In these lawless days,' he interrupted, 'a man should not even set out upon a boating expedition without means of protection,' and he slid an efficient-looking blade from within the cane.

Holmes smiled. 'Then I accept your gallant offer.'

At that moment the carriage swept round a corner, with Essex seated alongside its driver. It was a handsomely painted open carriage, drawn by two fine bays, and we were soon on board. Wiggins came up as we boarded.

'Shall I be off then, Mr Holmes?'

'Certainly not,' said Holmes. 'You may yet be useful to us. Climb in.'

The boy scrambled in and perched himself nervously between Binstead and Newnham-Davis. As Holmes instructed the driver and we made off, Binstead regarded the Cockney youth solemnly, Wiggins returning the gaze.

'Are you really Mr Binstead, the Pitcher of the Pink 'Un?' he asked at last.

'I have that very great honour,' said Binstead. 'And who are you, young man?'

'I'm Wiggins, sir, of the Baker Street Irregulars, but when I'm not helpin' Mr Holmes I sells the Pink 'Un.'

'Do you indeed?' exclaimed Binstead. 'Then you are a professional colleague, Mr Wiggins, and deserving of our hospitality. Dwarf, have a scramble in the luncheon basket and see if we can muster a bite for this young man.'

149

Very shortly Wiggins was regaling himself with a bottle of Codd's and a large portion of pie while Holmes gave our companions a brief outline of our quest.

'Shall we catch him, do you think?' I asked Binstead. 'He's had nearly half an hour's start.'

'With Gilbert at the whip, these wheels underneath us and those bays we should be able to catch up with a growler loaded with luggage,' he said. 'The problem may be if he changes course.'

Gilbert was indeed keeping up a good pace but it was not long before we approached a fork in the road. Holmes hailed an elderly road-mender who was solemnly tamping grit into hollows in the surface.

'Have you seen a dark red four-wheeler with luggage on top pass this way?'

'About twenty minutes gone,' said the old man and pointed towards the right fork. 'Going a fair speed and he went along that way.'

Holmes flung the man a coin and Gilbert whipped up the horses.

'He is not going south or south-east as I had expected,' mused Holmes. 'I had thought he would be making for the south coast to take a boat for the Continent.'

'He's heading for Wokingham or Reading,' said Binstead.

'Perhaps he's making for Broadmoor – seeking asylum, what?' said the Dwarf.

'He may make for Reading,' said Holmes. 'He can get Great Western and South Western trains from there. But where would he be going and why take this route? The Bath road would have been quicker from Windsor. No, it is not Reading.'

Mile after mile we rattled on, sometimes checking our direction from bystanders. Each time we learnt that we were gaining on our quarry but still we could not deduce his destination.

We followed him through byways and lanes to the south-east of Reading, passing through villages like Arborfield and Swallowfield. If our errand had not been so vital, I could have thoroughly enjoyed this spanking ride through pretty villages and lanes decked with midsummer flowers.

Beyond Swallowfield we reached a high road again. There was no convenient pedestrian to assist us and we drew up in bafflement.

'Do you know this road?' Holmes asked our companions.

'Certainly,' said Newnham-Davis. 'It's the road from Reading to Basingstoke.'

'He is not going to Reading,' said Holmes. 'It has to be Basingstoke. To the left, driver!'

'Basingstoke!' exclaimed the Dwarf. 'It's a very odd place for a murderer to flee to!'

'It is', said Binstead, 'a very odd place in any case. I went there once.'

'Quite sufficient!' said Newnham-Davis and the pair of comedians relapsed into silence.

A few miles further we climbed a ridge. From its top a long view of the countryside and the road ahead spread before us. Essex hollered from the box, 'We have him! He's up ahead!'

We all strained our eyes and, sure enough, at the very limit of the long straight stretch on which we found ourselves, we could see a dark red four-wheeler.

Gilbert plied his whip and drew extra effort from his splendid horses and all of us were cheered by the sight of our quarry. Now we knew we had taken the right turnings and were not chasing a wild goose.

We drew closer to Tumbletye's vehicle for a while, but suddenly he seemed to have recognised a pursuit and his own driver put on a burst of speed. Soon he was hidden from sight in a little cloud of dust and we were only keeping pace.

Holmes had sat forward when Essex called out, and he remained in that posture, hands clasped over the head of his stick, oblivious to the rocking of our vehicle. His magnificent eyes blazed as he peered ahead for a further sight of Tumbletye's carriage. Suddenly he sat upright and snapped his fingers.

'Of course!' he exclaimed. 'Basingstoke! He is going no further. At Basingstoke he has two railway lines – one to the south coast and the South Western line to Plymouth! This morning's paper announced that the Cunarder *Etruria* had cleared the London Docks for New York and will call at Plymouth tonight for mail and late passengers. He is escaping back to America. We must stop him before he boards that train!'

The pace turned in our favour as the weight of Tumbletye's carriage told and soon we had regained lost distance, but we were still far behind him and could only see him when the road opened out. I was partly raised in Hampshire and was now on familiar turf. I grew increasingly and uneasily aware that Basingstoke could not be very far ahead.

Our horses were now at full stretch and beginning to show the strain of the long racing pull, but it was impossible to let up on them for even a moment. Soon Basingstoke was in sight and Tumbletye's four-wheeler was vanishing into its streets.

As we reached the fringes of the town Gilbert asked, 'Which railway station, Mr Holmes?'

'The South Western,' replied Holmes immediately.

'Did you not say that he might be making for the Continent?' I said. 'If he is, the Great Western station will be the one. In an hour or so he can be on the south coast and take a boat across the Channel.'

'Quite right, Watson,' said Holmes, 'but why should he risk it when he may yet make the Plymouth boat train and reach the *Etruria* before she sails tonight? That way he will travel straight to New York. If he fails to catch the boat train, he can still try the Great Western line and make for France.'

We plunged into the streets of the little town, heedless of the danger to which we exposed innocent pedestrians and other travellers, Gilbert flinging our carriage around narrow corners with as much skill and aplomb as Johnny Burke had swung the Deadwood coach.

Making for the railway station we suddenly found our way impeded by an enormous brewer's dray emerging from the backyard of an inn. We sat, all drumming our fingers with impatience, as the dray's driver slowly turned his cumbersome vehicle leaving us the narrowest room to pass. Gilbert took the gap bravely, only scraping our paintwork as we passed the dray.

'Cost us a bob to the stable!' remarked Newnham-Davis.

'Worth every penny, Dwarf,' said Binstead, whose normally solemn face was alight with excitement and whose eyes glittered to match Holmes'.

At last we rattled into the yard of the London and South Western Railway's station. Tumbletye's equipage stood by the entrance, the luggage gone from its roof. The man himself was nowhere to be seen. From up the line a train whistled and the sound of its engine grew in our ears.

'The Plymouth boat train!' cried Holmes. 'Come, gentlemen!'

Together we leapt from our carriage and raced towards the station.

24

THE BATTLE OF BASINGSTOKE

We swarmed into the station's booking hall, our eyes turning in all directions as we sought a sign of our prey. The boy Wiggins and Essex made straight for the platform entrance, but a uniformed ticket-collector halted them.

'Carry on!' cried Binstead, who had brought up the rear of our column and was now at the ticket window. 'I have platform tickets for six.'

The railway functionary stood back and we poured on to the platform. A long train, evidently the Plymouth express, stood at the platform, several of its doors open, and we darted hither and yon along its length, peering into windows and jumping into open doorways to see if we could spy Tumbletye.

As I stepped down from one carriage I looked along the train, towards the guard's van at the rear. A considerable stack of luggage was still piled on the platform and porters were lifting items into the van as fast as they might. I was on the point of turning away when a flash of bright colours in the sunlight caught my eye from beyond the pile of luggage. I realised that I had caught a glimpse of Tumbletye's braided coat.

'Quick!' I called to Holmes. 'He is up there! By the guard's van!'

Holmes and I both made in that direction, but we were overtaken again by Wiggins and Essex.

'Have a care, lads!' shouted Holmes. 'He may have men with him – armed men!'

Whether the two heard him I know not, for they slackened speed not a whit until, when they were some twenty yards from the guard's van, two young men leapt out from a first-class carriage and confronted Essex and the lad.

That the two new arrivals were not first-class passengers was immediately evident and I needed no second glance to tell me that they were another two such as those that Holmes and I had bested outside Tumbletye's lodgings.

A hand-to-hand struggle was now in progress in which even little Wiggins was giving a remarkably good account of himself for his size, but I feared the production of what seemed to be Tumbletye's weapon of choice for his henchmen – the surgical knife. I felt in my pocket and pulled out my Adams .450.

As I advanced on the struggling foursome with pistol in hand, seeking the opportunity to fire a shot that might disable one of Tumbletye's ruffians without injuring our lads, Holmes caught my arm.

'No gunplay yet, Watson,' he commanded.

'But Holmes,' I protested, 'you know Tumbletye's men carry knives. I was trying to protect Essex and the boy.'

'If Tumbletye catches the express here,' said Holmes, 'we can have him stopped at Plymouth. His arrest here is not worth a death.'

'It is certainly not worth the death of young Wiggins or Essex,' I replied, hotly, and started forward again.

Holmes plucked my sleeve once more. 'If you are determined on firing,' he said, 'count five, then fire one shot well above their heads.'

No sooner had he spoken the words than he seemed to vanish from my side. I looked around, but saw no sign of him, and decided to follow his instruction though I had no idea what he had in mind.

After a rapid count of five I let fly a single shot, aimed well above the heads of the four strugglers. It had the effect which I imagine Holmes desired. The fight stopped for a moment, as all four looked to see whence the shot had come.

Before battle had recommenced, Holmes sprang from out of the deep shadows behind Tumbletye's men and thrust his stick sharply into the back of the lout who was belabouring Wiggins.

The ruffian spun round, abandoning Wiggins, and, seeing himself attacked by a six-foot adult, felt in his pocket. I feared that he was groping for a knife and I was right. A split second later the sun glinted on a blade in the scoundrel's right hand.

Wiggins had the good sense to withdraw from the fray, and was now bent, hands on knees, regaining his breath. Essex was giving a thoroughly good account of himself in an exchange of fists with his man. The second man, now armed, crouched and swept his knife out towards Holmes. With a graceful, curving movement, Holmes spun his stick, and I saw a bright flash in the air as the blade concealed within it was exposed for action.

Behind me Newnham-Davis and Binstead had emerged from the train.

'I say, Pitcher,' said the Dwarf, 'Holmes and Essex are getting all the fun. Join in, shall we?'

'If you say so, Mr Editor,' said Binstead, and he too extracted the blade of his swordstick.

'Steady the Buffs!' cried Newnham-Davis and he and Pitcher trotted down the platform to join the fray.

Battered by Essex on one hand, attacked with a blade by Holmes on another, Tumbletye's minders now saw, over their shoulders, two more six-footers, one armed with a sword-stick, bearing down upon them. Their kind of brute is a handy fighter when the odds are in favour, but they now knew themselves outnumbered. They cut and ran for the exit, Holmes taking advantage of their disarray to slash one of them across his knife-hand sending the weapon skittering across the platform.

Binstead and Newnham-Davis came to a halt. Holmes strolled towards them and I joined the group as Wiggins and Essex came up.

'Well done, gentlemen,' said Holmes. 'We have now only to deal with Dr Tumbletye. Do we yet know where he is?'

'Not on the train,' said Binstead.

'I spotted him beyond the luggage,' I said. 'I haven't seen him since.'

'I slipped out through the Parcels Office and back through the cattle gate,' said Holmes. 'He was not outside. He must still be within the station. We must search.'

We were about to renew our search when the stationmaster hurried up.

'I do not know what you gentlemen believe you are doing,' he said, 'but unless you have an extremely good explanation for the firing of a pistol and the brandishing of weapons on my plat-form, I shall be forced to call the police.'

156

Holmes smiled. 'I am Sherlock Holmes,' he said, presenting his card, 'and this is my friend and colleague, Dr Watson. These other gentlemen are assisting us in a matter of some consequence to Scotland Yard. If you wish to invoke the police, may I suggest that you wire to Inspector Lestrade at the Yard?'

The railway official seemed a little mollified. He looked at Holmes' card and signalled urgently to the guard of the Plymouth train. Doors slammed along its length, the guard's whistle blew, and almost imperceptibly the train began to slip away along the platform.

'Tell me,' asked Holmes of the stationmaster, 'have you seen a tall American, with bright yellow hair and bushy moustaches, somewhat theatrically dressed?'

'Why, yes, Mr Holmes. He arrived just before your party and took a first-class single to Plymouth.'

Holmes smiled at the confirmation of his deductions. 'And do you know where he might be now?' he asked.

The stationmaster shook his head. 'His two men brought a lot of luggage in for the guard's van. Last I saw of him was by the van supervising them. He must be on the train. All his trunks went on the train.'

'Perhaps you are right,' said Holmes and began to walk towards the entrance to the platform. He paused for a moment and said, 'If he is on the train we can have him stopped at Plymouth. There is nothing more to do here, gentlemen.'

He left the platform, and the rest of us followed. I caught up with him in the booking hall.

'Look here, Holmes,' I protested. 'I thought we agreed that Tumbletye isn't on the train. Suppose he's sneaked off to the Great Western station – he'll be away to France in no time.'

'Tush, Watson,' he remonstrated. 'You do not think that I abandon my prey so readily, do you? Tumbletye has had no opportunity to leave this station since you saw him. If Binstead and Newnham-Davis are right when they say that he was not on the train, then he is still here.'

'Then what do you propose?'

'To draw him out, Watson. What else? Wiggins,' he said, 'kindly position yourself by this door where you can keep an eye along the platform in both directions. I suggest you pay particular attention in that direction,' and he pointed. 'If you spot our man, we shall be outside in the carriage.'

Wiggins saluted and moved to his post while we strolled out to the carriage. We sat and smoked a while.

'If I were Tumbletye,' said Essex after a bit, 'I'd lay pretty low in whatever hidey-hole I'd found and stay there till the next Plymouth train.'

'So would I,' said Holmes, 'but you are not Tumbletye and neither am I. He is a man of a nervous and excitable disposition, not the kind that waits patiently. He believes that we are gone. He will soon emerge from hiding to confirm his impression.'

He had hardly spoken the words when Wiggins appeared at the station entrance, beckoning urgently.

Once again we piled out of Gilbert's carriage and into the station. Wiggins reported quickly to Holmes. 'He come out of the Gents, Mr Holmes. He's sitting on a bench down there,' and he pointed. 'Between here and the Parcels Office.'

'Well done!' said Holmes. 'Watson, Essex, come with me! Can the rest of you simply block the Parcels Office entrance and the cattle gate so that he can't escape us that way?'

They moved to their posts and Essex and I followed Holmes on to the platform.

'Good evening, Dr Tumbletye,' called Holmes as we approached him.

He looked up, sprang to his feet and backed away. 'You cannot interfere with me, Holmes,' he cried, in his high, slightly cracked voice. 'I have done nothing that you can prove.'

'Oh, but you have,' said Holmes. 'You boasted to Watson and me of your intentions – '

'I never said what they were,' interrupted Tumbletye.

'Watson and I have seen what they were, Tumbletye,' said my friend. 'So has Colonel Cody and others. You must have been aware before you left Windsor that your plot had failed. Two of your assassins are dead, but the third lives and will, I feel sure, see the wisdom of giving evidence against you.'

He moved towards Tumbletye who backed yet further, towards the open door of the Parcels Office. Reaching inside his jacket he brandished the knife that I had last seen spinning away across the platform from the hand of his henchman.

'Keep away!' he screamed. 'You'll never take me, Holmes!'

'The stationmaster here is most anxious to have no further violence on his platform,' said Holmes evenly, and as he spoke I saw movement in the shadows of the Parcels Office.

Tumbletye began to flail the air in a circular motion with the knife, an inexpert use of the weapon but sufficiently dangerous to hold us back. Holmes quietly unsheathed his blade again and stepped towards the mad American.

Tumbletye yelped, tried to step back a pace, and fell sprawling over Wiggins, who had crept silently from the Parcels Office and knelt behind the madman's feet. Once again the knife went skittering across the pavement, but this time Wiggins took it into his custody as Holmes laid the point of his blade against Tumbletye's throat.

The stationmaster ran up, dismay written all over his face, as Holmes solemnly intoned, 'I arrest you, Francis Tumbletye, for conspiracy to murder Edward, Prince of Wales, and the Kings of Greece, Norway, Belgium and Denmark.'

This litany seemed to impress the stationmaster, for he was all at our disposal when Holmes turned to him and asked, 'Do you, by any chance, have a length of stout cord, stationmaster?'

25

KNAVISH TRICKS

Once Tumbletye was securely bound we laid him on the floor of our carriage, where he lay and cursed so fluently that even Wiggins turned pink and we were forced to threaten the American into silence.

We did not feel able to demand more of Gilbert's fine horses after their exertions on the road from Windsor, but Holmes suggested that, while the horses were rested and refreshed, we should take refreshment ourselves as his guests. Accordingly we found a pleasant inn and, while the horses were tended by the tavern's grooms, our party, including Gilbert and Wiggins, spread itself around a table inside the house.

'I must congratulate you,' said Holmes to Gilbert, as we addressed a large rabbit pie. 'Your driving today has been superb.'

''Tis nothing, Mr Holmes,' he replied. 'I have been drivin' Mr Binstead about a few years now and I know as he requires the best.'

'Mr Holmes,' said Essex, 'do I get my story?'

'Story?' exclaimed Pitcher. 'You're not going to let this Yankee whippersnapper take away the bread from the mouths of poor British journalists?'

Holmes let his eye rove silently over Binstead's very solid form and the platter of rabbit pie that lay in front of him before replying.

'Whether there is a "story", gentlemen, depends very much on Scotland Yard,' he said. 'Listen for a moment to the conversations around us. Do you hear outraged and excited comment on this afternoon's events at Windsor? No – despite the fact that there has been ample time for information about the incident to spread.'

'You believe the Yard has killed the story?' said Essex.

'It is evident, I believe, that they have not revealed what happened at the Wild West Show. It is not for nothing that Littlechild's men are known as the Secret Department. The Yard has a penchant for secrecy in any case and I imagine that they have found good reasons for suppressing news of Tumbletye's plot.'

'What good reasons might there be?' I asked.

'Oh, they will think of something,' said Holmes. 'They will say that news of the incident might mar the celebration tomorrow, that it might provoke anti-Irish demonstrations or even,' and he smiled at Essex, 'anti-American demonstrations. There is nothing so fertile as the mind of a British public servant seeking reasons to cloak his own or his Department's failures. Whether there is a story for you to argue about, gentlemen, will rest entirely upon Scotland Yard's willingness to admit its shortcomings in this affair.'

'But if they try Tumbletye,' I said, 'it will be bound to come out.'

'Indeed,' said Holmes, 'and then you will have a story. Until then you do not.'

'Hang Scotland Yard!' exclaimed Newnham-Davis. He grasped his glass and stood. 'Gentlemen, I give you a toast – Her Gracious Majesty Queen Victoria!'

We rose, glasses in hand, and Binstead quoted, 'Scatter her enemies, confound their politics, frustrate their knavish tricks!' before we drank the Dwarf's toast.

Binstead raised his glass. 'I give you Mr Sherlock Holmes!' he cried, but Holmes demurred.

'No, no, Binstead. I have merely applied my professional skills to the problems of a private client which happened to bring me to Tumbletye. You should toast yourselves for your courage and enthusiasm in helping me to bring the matter to a successful conclusion.'

'Very well then,' said the Pitcher, 'I give you young Wiggins who personally brought about the downfall of Tumbletye!'

We drank while the boy sat and blushed. After the toast Holmes fumbled in his pocket.

'I am reminded', he said, 'that we have taken no steps to ensure that our prisoner does not starve. Wiggins, will you be good enough to take him something to eat and drink?'

'Not rabbit pie,' declared Binstead, firmly. 'Fenians do not deserve rabbit pie. Take him bread and cheese, lad.'

Wiggins went off and we continued to take our ease. After the considerable exertions of that day, it was a real pleasure to lounge in congenial company over good food and drink. Binstead demonstrated the reason for his sobriquet, reciting stories of the ring, the music hall and the race course, and Holmes contributed anecdotes of his profession, while Newnham-Davis drew on his activities in camp and battle as well as on the stage to keep us amused.

It was some little time before we realised that Wiggins had not returned to the table.

'It is no matter,' said Holmes rising. 'It is time we were leaving. We shall all wish to be up betimes for tomorrow's activities and I have a prisoner to deliver to Cannon Row yet.'

He paid our reckoning and we strolled out together into the inn's courtyard. It was dark, but with that luminous darkness of midsummer. There was no sign of Wiggins that we could see.

As we waited for Gilbert to harness the horses, a train whistle sounded as another express approached the station. Stepping into our carriage, Newnham-Davis let out a muttered oath.

As we followed him we could see, even in the gloom of the innyard, that the figure that lay, kicking and wriggling, in the well of the carriage was too short to be Tumbletye. It was Wiggins, thoroughly bound with cord and gagged with his own neckerchief.

Swiftly Holmes cut the boy free with his pocket-knife. Wiggins was in tears, but they soon proved to be marks of rage and humiliation not of hurt.

'I'm sorry, Mr Holmes,' he spluttered, once the gag was removed. 'I brought him his bread and cheese and he asked me to untie one of his hands so he could eat. I saw no harm, so I did that. When he'd had his scoff he grabbed me by the throat – nearly choked me, he did. I tried to get him off of me with the knife what was in me pocket, but he took it off me and said he'd cut me throat.'

'He would have done so, my boy,' said Holmes. 'You were lucky to escape.'

'Where has he gone?' I asked.

'To Plymouth,' asserted Holmes. 'Did you not hear the western express arrive a few moments ago?'

'Will he catch the *Etruria*?' said Essex.

'She will not sail till the morning tide,' said Holmes. 'He has ample time to board her, but we have ample time to wire Lestrade and have him stopped.'

'Hang it!' ejaculated Newnham-Davis. 'We're not letting him get away now! Come on, Watson!'

He sprang away and I followed. Together we pounded down the street towards the railway station but neither of us was helped in our effort by the size of our dinner or the quantity of drink taken. The Dwarf drew ahead of me and, by the time he reached the station's entrance, I was labouring several yards behind. Even at that distance I could hear the slamming of doors along the train and the guard's long blast on his whistle that signified that we were too late.

I reached the booking hall in time to see Newnham-Davis vault the ticket gate and sprint along the platform but the Plymouth train was already well on its way and he never stood a chance of catching up with it. He turned away as the red light at the rear of the train dwindled away down the line, and walked slowly back to join me at the gate, muttering fierce curses in between his panting breaths.

Back at the inn, Holmes was the only member of the party who seemed entirely unruffled by Tumbletye's escape.

'It would have amused me', he said, 'to have presented him in person to Scotland Yard, but they will catch him at Plymouth and Littlechild will not be able to deny that the capture is entirely due to our efforts.'

He drew out his watch. 'The evening telegraph service will have shut,' he said, 'and I had better not disturb the stationmaster again. Perhaps, Gilbert, you will be kind enough to stop at the police station. I imagine that the Hampshire police will allow me the courtesy of a wire to the Yard.'

Once that small task was completed we left Basingstoke, all the merriment and self-congratulation of our dinner-party evaporated despite Holmes' assurances.

163

Wiggins sat hunched in a corner of the carriage, his pale face streaked with tears, still evidently blaming himself for Tumbletye's escape.

'Cheer up, my lad,' said Binstead, after a while. 'We of the journalist's profession know that, try as we might, we cannot always secure the stories we want. We have to accept our failures with our successes.'

'But I ain't a journalist,' sniffed Wiggins. 'I'm a paper-boy who's the Captain of Mr Holmes' Irregulars and I spoiled it all, didn't I?'

'Would you like to be a journalist?' asked Binstead.

For the first time since we had left Basingstoke the hapless lad looked up.

'Wouldn't I just!' he said. 'But there's no chance for the likes of me.'

'Can you read and write?' asked the Pitcher.

'Yes,' said the boy, and I smiled at the recollection of his notes to Holmes. 'Well, mostly – not difficult words like.'

'Then, if you are willing to learn to read and write even more than mostly, you shall become that most despised of creatures in the press, an office boy at the Pink 'Un.'

'Oh, Mr Binstead,' said Wiggins, 'can I really?' He stopped short and looked across at Holmes. 'But what shall I do about the Irregulars? If Mr Holmes still wants me, I mean to say?'

Holmes smiled. 'Lose my trusted Captain of Irregulars? Certainly not, Wiggins. But if you wish to take Mr Binstead's very generous offer I would strongly recommend it.'

'I see no difficulty,' said Binstead. 'When Mr Holmes requires your skills he will find you that much more easily if he knows you're humping coal, filling ink-pots and carrying messages for me.'

'Then I accept,' said Wiggins.

Binstead shook him solemnly by the hand. 'Welcome to the Pink 'Un,' he said. 'Here's your first week's screw so you can get some shirts and collars and a pair of black boots. Take the rest of this week off and enjoy the Jubilee and be at the office, eight sharp, next Monday.'

I was grateful to Pitcher for cheering the boy up, let alone offering him some kind of future, for the shadow departed from

164

young Wiggins' features and for the remainder of our journey he listened in wide-eyed awe as Binstead outlined the duties of an office boy to him.

I was more than ready for my bed when we finally reached Baker Street. I could not recall a more strenuous day of alarms and exertions, but as I fell asleep I could not suppress a sneaking feeling that Holmes' confidence might be misplaced and that the story of Dr Tumbletye might not yet be over.

26

SOME MISCHIEF

The next day was, of course, Her Majesty's Golden Jubilee. From before daylight the streets of the city were paved with loyal Londoners and visitors from other parts of the nation, come to see their Queen ride to a triumphant celebration of her fifty years on the throne and to cheer her on her way.

'There is', observed Holmes, as we watched the royal procession pass, 'an aspect of popular thought that I find singularly difficult to fathom, Watson.'

'Really?' I said.

'Yes. Here we have a Queen who, shortly after her accession and ever since, has been criticised for having favourites – both in her own household and among politicians; a Queen who married a foreigner who was never popular with the public; who was criticised for burdening the public purse by the size of her family; a Queen who was widely and loudly attacked when she withdrew into mourning at her Consort's death, giving impetus to a Republican movement. But now – by the mere accident that she has survived half a century as our monarch – she is cheered through the streets by the same people who gossiped about her favourites, sneered at her husband, sang bawdy songs about the size of her family and loudly said that, if there was not to be a Republic, she should abdicate in favour of Prince Edward. Do you not find that extraordinary, Watson?'

'Now that you mention it, Holmes, yes.'

He shook his head. 'I count myself a believer in democracy, Watson, but sometimes I wonder if the extension of the franchise is such a good idea. What will become of Britain if the franchise is extended, Watson, to include the fickle and sentimental creatures who line the streets today?'

At the time I was much engaged in watching the spectacle before us, and paid Holmes' forebodings little attention, but in the thirty years that have passed his remarks have sometimes returned to my mind, never more so than now, when there is talk of extending the franchise to females after the war ends.

In the excitement of the Jubilee celebrations I lost sight of our involvement with Tumbletye for days. It was not until Holmes and I fulfilled our intention of visiting Cody's show that the matter came to my attention again.

We had gone along to Kensington in company with Wiggins and the Baker Street Irregulars, where we had seen the entire show in a great deal more comfort and with a lot less to distract us than at Windsor Castle. Colonel Cody had made the Irregulars passengers in the Deadwood stagecoach and, as the charade unfolded before me, I thought back a few days to the lawn at Windsor, to real shots flying and dead men falling.

Afterwards we met many of Cody's company and shared their meal and their camp-fire. It was as we packed the last drowsy Irregular into a crowded cab and took our farewells of Cody that he mentioned Tumbletye.

'I hear that there may be no case against Dr Tumbletye,' he said.

'Really?' said Holmes. 'Why should there not be?'

'Lestrade tells me that the only witness is dead,' said the American.

'The only witness?' said Holmes. 'You mean the assassin who survived at Windsor?'

'The same,' said Cody. 'Inspector Lestrade says that they had to operate to extract a bullet and your man died under the knife.'

Holmes turned sharply to me. 'Was it not your opinion, Watson, that the man would survive with adequate care?'

'Entirely,' I confirmed. 'What is more, there was no wound that would require a bullet to be extracted. I observed two wounds, both with clear indications that a bullet had passed right through the man's body. In neither case was there the least indication that any vital organ might have been damaged.'

'I have often criticised you, Watson, for failing to understand what your observations mean, but not in the field of medicine. In that area I have long been aware that you are accurate in your observations and properly cautious in any diagnosis which you make. There is some mischief here.'

The next morning at Baker Street Holmes seemed distracted. He ate little at breakfast and showed less than his usual enthusiasm for the morning papers until at last I asked what concerned him.

'Tumbletye,' he said. 'We have heard nothing further since I wired Lestrade from Basingstoke apart from Cody's story of the assassin's remarkable death.'

In a little while he wired Lestrade again, but no reply was forthcoming during that day and the little detective made no appearance at our lodgings.

It was more than a week before we heard further, a week during which I had grave difficulty in persuading my friend to avoid the attractions of his cocaine bottle. At last there came a morning when a familiar step sounded on the stair and Mrs Hudson showed Lestrade into our sitting-room.

Holmes made the Scotland Yard man welcome, but I was aware of a grim set to my friend's mouth, as I noted a certain uneasiness on Lestrade's part.

When we were settled Holmes looked directly at Lestrade.

'You had my wire?' he demanded.

'Yes,' said the little man. 'Yes, Mr Holmes. I had hoped to be here sooner but there are still duties connected with the Jubilee to be seen to.'

'I understand', said Holmes, 'that the American arrested at Windsor has died.'

'Yes,' said Lestrade. 'That is unfortunately so, Mr Holmes. I don't know all the particulars but I believe that it was thought necessary to remove a bullet to save his life and that the operation was not successful.'

'When was this?' asked Holmes.

'Only the next day,' said Lestrade. 'The very day of the Jubilee. It was most unfortunate, because it left us without a witness, of course.'

'I am a witness,' said Holmes, 'Watson is a witness, Colonel Cody is a witness, his stagecoach driver, Burke, is a witness.'

'As to what took place at Windsor, yes,' said Lestrade, awkwardly, 'but that would only be against the man himself not against Dr Tumbletye.'

'Watson and I', said Holmes, 'heard from Tumbletye's own lips a statement of his intentions to strike a blow against Britain and America on the eve of the Jubilee.'

Lestrade turned his hat in his hands, uncomfortably. 'Very circumstantial, I'm sure you'll agree, Mr Holmes.'

'Circumstantial evidence has been quite good enough to hang people in this country, for a long time,' said Holmes. 'Besides, Tumbletye is unstable and a dramatic braggart. What has he said under questioning? Has he made no stupid admissions?'

Lestrade looked out of the window, his sallow features unnaturally pale. 'He is not', he said at last, 'actually in our custody.'

'You lost him at Plymouth?' snapped Holmes. 'How on earth did that happen?'

Lestrade shifted uneasily on his seat. 'Mr Holmes,' he said, 'this matter has been under the control of Mr Littlechild and the Secret Department. Now, you know what manner of man is Mr Littlechild. It was his decision that, without the evidence of the cowboy from Windsor, there was no case against Tumbletye.'

Even I could see that Lestrade had walked straight into the trap which Holmes had set. My friend stared at the Scotland Yarder with an expression almost of contempt.

'Lestrade,' he said, softly, 'I have never accounted logic one of your strong points, but even you must have difficulty understanding how, on Monday night when Tumbletye was *en route* for Plymouth, Littlechild was able to take a decision not to arrest him because of the death of a potential witness on Tuesday.'

Lestrade's jaw dropped and he sat silent, still twisting his hat in his hands.

'No, Lestrade,' continued my friend. 'The death of the American, if he is indeed dead, had nothing to do with it. Littlechild was merely anxious to protect the reputation of his Department, to permit no trial in which the facts of the event at Windsor would become public property. He would rather let a murderous madman escape – again!'

'Again?' echoed Lestrade.

'It is virtually certain that Tumbletye was involved in the murders of Cavendish and Burke in Dublin and that he fled from Ireland when they were done. But he did not stay away from Britain, he returned to execute his Jubilee plot. Now he has fled again, but mark my words, Lestrade, he will return and when he does you may not know his intentions and he may succeed in some outrage that, if it occurs, should properly be laid at Littlechild's door.'

Lestrade got up. 'I don't think that's entirely fair to Mr Little-child,' he began, but Holmes stopped him with an imperious gesture.

'I do not blame you, Lestrade. You have been Littlechild's cat's-paw in this. You must take your orders. But I do not have to take orders and when Tumbletye returns to this shore do not come to me for assistance.'

The little detective left, crestfallen, and Holmes sat, eyes blazing and fingers drumming for several minutes. Then he reached for his violin and passed an hour in those exercises which delighted him and seemed to soothe his nerves though they did little for mine.

'I suggest', he remarked, as he laid down his instrument, 'that if I become too vainglorious of my success, Watson, you should remember to whisper one word to me – Basingstoke!'

It is right that I should record that my friend's prediction was borne out. Little more than a year later Tumbletye was back in London. Once again the Secret Department at the Yard exercised themselves in trying to determine his intentions, once more without success. If Littlechild had learned anything by his failure to drive the madman away from Britain it seemed to be that Tumbletye must be frightened into never returning.

In December 1888, Tumbletye was charged with an unnatural offence and set free on bail. True to form, he fled the country forthwith, returning to America. Littlechild's men pursued him across the Atlantic, where they told the American press that they had pursued, not a Fenian conspirator, but the maniac who had perpetrated the East End murders – the so-called 'Jack the Ripper'! It seemed to do the trick. I never heard any further word of Tumbletye's presence in Britain.

It is also right that, in chronicling Holmes' efforts in this matter and his own view that his enquiry was unsuccessful, I should record my own failure. The excitements of the enquiry had so taken over my thoughts that I ignored Newnham-Davis's exhortation to back Merry Hampton for the Jubilee Derby, which it won handsomely – at considerable profit to the wise.

And our client – John Byron? Not long after the Jubilee Holmes received a cheque from him, accompanied by a short note. It thanked my friend for his efforts and congratulated him on preventing Tumbletye's plot. It also confirmed that the writer was leaving England but did not reveal his destination. I recall that it ended, 'Remember me, Mr Holmes, as a Confederate, paying the penalty upon his own responsibility.' Sometimes when my mind returns to our adventures of thirty years ago I remember poor Booth – for I believe that Byron was indeed the assassin of Lincoln and I know that Holmes believed it. If it were not bad enough for a patriot of his burning zeal to be lured into the planning of cynical traitors to the Union and made both a cat's-paw of their devious plots and a traitor to his own cause, to be doomed to roam the world under a false identity, bereft of family, friends and nation, must be a fearful doom. I can only hope that he has found his peace now.

EDITOR'S NOTES

As with the earlier Watson manuscripts which I have edited for publication, I have made such researches as I have been able, both to elucidate references in his text and, if possible, to establish the authenticity of the document.

The fruits of my researches are recorded in these notes, though I have little doubt that they are incomplete and it may well be that further enquiry into some of the matters noted might be pursued with profit.

CHAPTER ONE

As to Watson's age, we can be fairly certain that Watson was born in 1852 and Holmes in 1854. This and the other manuscripts in my possession seem to have been written in the latter stages of the Great War or immediately after. Watson describes himself as being in his 'seventh decade' and he would have been sixty-five or sixty-six in 1917/18. Unhappily no one seems to be certain of the dates of death of either Holmes or Watson. Some give 1929 as the year of Watson's death, while others assert that he was still alive in the 1940s. W. S. Baring Gould states as a fact that Holmes died on 6 January 1957, his longevity being attributable to fifty years of taking royal jelly produced by his bees (*Sherlock Holmes: A Biography of the World's First Consulting Detective*, Hart-Gibbon, 1962; Panther Books, 1975).

The Aberdeen University legend of the execution of the porter Downie is an old and well known one. Many ex-students have referred to it in memoirs of their student days, though there is no record of any such event actually having occurred. Some thirty years ago, Sandy Hobbs of the University of Strathclyde published a paper on the legend in the course of his pioneering studies of urban legends in Britain. Oddly, the Girl Guides have a ritual game which revolves around the theme of someone being convinced that they are to be beheaded and having a playing card drawn across their neck.

The song about Holmes seems likely to have been the following:

Sherlock Holmes

I would indite this ditty to a man who's very cute,
He's the terror of Bill Sloggins and them who'd do a scoot;
He can tell you where you've been to just by looking at your
    boot,
And you'll know him by the name of Sherlock Holmes.

Chorus: With his lips hard set and a cigarette,
    As his fingers through his hair he combs,
    He's never yet been baffled,
    And he's sent 'em to the scaffold
    By the score, has Sherlock Holmes.

I asked him out to dine at my place near Kempton Park,
I said the wine was Ruinart, I'd shifted every mark;
'You lie! It's three-and-sixpenny, I know it by the cork,
For I've found it on the floor,' said Sherlock Holmes.

One summer day we started for a race course close to town,
He said 'against the favourite'; we planked our utmost
    'brown';
And before the race was over, why, the favourite he broke
    down –
'That physic's done the trick,' said Sherlock Holmes.

He asked a few pals up one night; at poker we did play;
The stakes were high, the end drew nigh – this great man was
    no jay –
Five aces on the table, with a pistol, he did lay –
'I shall now collect the oof,' said Sherlock Holmes.

You say it is a pity that this splendid man should die.
I think the Swiss tale is a plant, I'll give my reason why.

There's a lady in the question, so he's gone and done a 'guy',
But he'll turn up again, will Sherlock Holmes.

Chorus: With his lips hard set and a cigarette,
    As his fingers through his hair he combs,
    He's never yet been baffled,
    And he'll send 'em to the scaffold
    By the score, will Sherlock Holmes.

The reference to poker seems to identify this as the song in question, though there are a number of other songs about Holmes. This one appears with its music in *The Scottish Students' Song Book*, 6th edition (Bayley and Ferguson, London and Glasgow, 1897), where it is identified as the work of Claude Ralston who was, apparently, a Writer to the Signet (the Scottish equivalent of a solicitor) in Edinburgh and 'author of many songs of great popularity in Edinburgh circles'.

While the song presents a highly individual picture of Holmes as a race-horse doping, card-sharping, thieving womaniser, its author must nevertheless be given credit for predicting that Holmes would rise again from the Reichenbach Falls. Others have implied or stated that Holmes' three-year disappearance was connected with a woman. Baring Gould, in the work cited above, states as fact that Holmes used the occasion to meet Irene Adler ('the woman') in Montenegro where their affair led to the birth of a son. Unless Holmes lied ruthlessly to Watson (a barely considerable situation) this was impossible. In 'A Scandal in Bohemia' Watson tells us that Holmes admired Irene Adler's intellect, but also that she was dead within three years of that case, i.e. before Holmes vanished.

Recent changes in British copyright law have brought to life formerly extinct rights and certain deceased authors are now reaching out from their graves to claw percentages from their successors. If, in quoting the above song, I have infringed an existing copyright, I apologise and plead ignorance of the date of the lawyer's death.

Like Holmes, I am not a card-player, but *The Encyclopaedia of Sports, Games and Pastimes* (Fleetway House, London, 1935) informs me that at poker a 'royal flush' is a hand consisting of the ace to ten of any suit. That seems to be an English definition – events described by Watson suggest that Americans use the phrase for four kings and an ace.

'The Reigate Squires' story appeared in America as 'The Reigate Squire', American editors finding some offensive connotation in 'squires'. Even 'squire' was not innocent, for the American title eventually became 'The Reigate Puzzle'.

Dolly Williamson was the nickname of Adolphus Williamson, head of the Criminal Investigation Department at Scotland Yard. He had a reputation as an excellent detective, but at this period was suffering ill health and the difficulties of a Department still depleted after the corruption scandal in the CID a few years before (see my notes to *Sherlock Holmes and the Devil's Grail*, Constable, 1995). Littlechild was the head of the Secret Department, formed in the early 1880s, and later known as the Special Branch.

I am grateful to the United States Embassy Information Service for confirming that the American Minister to London in 1887 was indeed Edward J. Phelps. An unforgiving memory of the War of Independence and the War of 1812 denied the United States an Ambassador at the Court of Saint James. That dignity was only granted in 1895.

Where, by the way, did Holmes first meet Buffalo Bill Cody? It is to be hoped that Watson succeeded in extracting that story from Holmes and recording it for posterity.

CHAPTER THREE

What was unusual about Watson's second name? Many Holmesian scholars have spotted that, although Watson styles himself as 'John H. Watson', his wife called him 'James'. Dorothy Sayers put forward the interesting theory that Watson's middle name was the Scots 'Hamish' and that his wife Anglicised it into 'James' as a pet name.

CHAPTER FOUR

If we cannot be certain of Watson's middle name, it is always a relief when he gives up disguising the identities of people and inserts a real name, which he never did in his published records. However, no longer writing for immediate publication, he does, in the present manuscripts, name identifiable characters. Littlechild's suspect, the strangely moustached Doctor, was real and his career was as Lestrade describes, but it was, in fact, much more bizarre than Lestrade seems to have known.

Tumbletye was a larger than life character known all over America and elsewhere. Making as much as $15,000 per year from his quack treatments, he was also driven out of cities where he had been exposed, and pursued by people who believed he had conned them. A coroner's jury probing the death of one of his patients found him guilty of manslaughter by his 'atrocious treatment', but took so long that he had fled the jurisdiction.

His arrest in the Lincoln case seems to have arisen because he used the alias 'J. H. Blackburn'. There was a real Dr Blackburn, a Confederate agent called Luke Pryor Blackburn. In 1865 the Assistant Secretary for War of the United States ordered Blackburn's arrest, after an allegation that he had been involved in a plan to ship blankets infected with yellow fever from Bermuda to New York. Although the military authorities holding Tumbletye soon satisfied themselves that he was not a part of the assassination conspiracy, the Assistant Secretary suggested that he should be held in a penitentiary and questioned about his knowledge of the conspirators. He was, however, released and published a book called *Kidnapping of Dr Tumbletye, By Order of the Secretary of War of the US*.

A skilful self-advertiser, when a music hall presented a sketch about him it was alleged that he was the actor in the sketch. Nevertheless, he sued the music hall for defamation!

Mackay Lomasney was an American Fenian who, together with a man named Fleming, was totally destroyed when a bomb which they were trying to place under the southern end of London Bridge blew them and their boat to untraceable fragments. 'Kelly' appears to be a reference to Captain T. J. Kelly, an American Civil War officer who assisted the Fenians in the 1867 revolt. He was arrested after an explosion at Clerkenwell Prison, where his second-in-command, Captain Richard O'Sullivan Burke, was being held. Burke was also a Civil War veteran.

The Labouchere Amendment was a section which the Liberal MP and editor Labouchere succeeded in adding to the otherwise uncontroversial Criminal Law Amendment Act of 1885. It made homosexual acts in private a serious criminal offence. It has been suggested that the measure was intended as a warning shot across the bows of Prince Albert Victor, Duke of Clarence and eldest son of the Prince of Wales. In 1889 Clarence was named in American newspapers as being involved with a male brothel in London.

CHAPTER FIVE

The quaintly named Cuckolds' Point is, according to the guides on the Thames tourist boats, named in memory of a boat-builder whose yard was nearby and who suspected his wife of, or detected her in, marital infidelity. To discourage her, he constructed a ducking-stool as used in the past to punish scolding women and witches and ducked her in the river. This action was greatly admired by his friends and neighbours, who soon began to contract him to deal with their own faithless wives for a price. I have to point out that the Thames river-boat guides have fertile imaginations and there is probably some far more prosaic explanation of the name.

The calculation of time of drowning by fleas was a method more precise than any that has been applied since public hygiene made fleas less prolific. Fleas are extremely difficult to drown. If placed in water they go into a state of suspended animation which can last for very long periods. Corpses from the river were searched for fleas and those found would be placed upon a saucer and the time noted. The time at which they revived would also be noted. Because a flea takes exactly as long to become active again as it has spent in the water, it was possible to gauge the time of death with great accuracy.

Holmes' knowledge of tattoos was encyclopaedic. According to Baring Gould (see above), Holmes' first book was *Upon Tattoo Marks*, privately printed in London in 1878 and including 'one of the first scholarly examinations of the pigments used extensively by Japanese and Chinese artists'.

That American sailors wore a rabbit tattooed on their foot as a charm against drowning is remarked by Stan Hugill in his *Sailortown* (Routledge and Kegan Paul Ltd, 1967). British seamen preferred a baby's caul in a sealed bag worn around the neck. Unscrupulous seaport traders sold the sealed bags with fake cauls inside, and when a sailor wearing a bag drowned his messmates would remark that he must have been wearing 'a Jew's caul'.

That the American custom is still extant is noted in Denis Healey's *The Time of My Life* (Michael Joseph, 1989). He mentions that his American journalist friend Paul Jacobs wore a tattoo on his ankle as a charm against drowning, though in Jacobs' case it was a fish.

CHAPTER SIX

The surviving records of the Confederate Navy do not reveal any Ashley Tremaille, though he might have enlisted under a *nom de guerre*. There were many Britons on both sides in America's Civil War, both as emigrants in the Union and the Confederacy and as soldiers (and sailors) of fortune. For example, Captain John Clibbon Brain, CSN, who was both the last Confederate ship's commander to surrender and the last Confederate kept a prisoner-of-war, was an Englishman. Although he was born in London, his family home was (curiously) at Nailsworth in Gloucestershire. He cannot have been Watson's 'Ashley Tremaille'. Brain lived on until 1923 and left family in America according to *The Last of the Confederate Privateers* by D. and J. Hay (Paul Harris Publishing, Edinburgh, 1977).

CHAPTER SEVEN

The Invincibles were a splinter group of American-funded Fenian assassins who, in 1882, murdered Lord Frederick Cavendish, the newly appointed Secretary of State, and Thomas Burke, his Permanent Secretary, in broad daylight in Phoenix Park, Dublin. The attack was directed at Burke, whom the Invincibles called a 'Castle rat' – an Irish Catholic who served the English administration at Dublin Castle. Cavendish was killed because he intervened. The weapons used in the attack were surgical knives.

In the wake of the murders, twenty-six of the forty or so Invincibles turned informer and five were hanged. Two Americans were said to have fled from Dublin. I have not been able to confirm whether one of them was Dr Tumbletye. One of the informers was sent to Australia afterwards, but that convict-born country refused him permission to land. Another died insane, while a third was assassinated in South Africa. For a detailed account of the assassination and the arrest and trial of the Invincibles, see *Irish Conspiracies*, Frederick M. Bussy (Everett, London, 1910).

CHAPTER EIGHT

Colonel Pericles Craig appears under a fictitious name, but his function as described by Watson is interesting. He appears to have been a 'Presidential Agent'. These functionaries date back to somewhere immediately after the Civil War and very little has ever been revealed about them. In the 1940s Upton Sinclair included a volume called *Presidential Agent* in his eleven-novel sequence *World's End* (Werner Laurie, London 1940–1952). His hero, Lanny Budd, is appointed as 'PA 103' by Franklin Roosevelt and carries out several missions reporting directly to the President. This seems an unlikely scenario. In the 1960s it emerged that there were then six Presidential Agents, one based in the USA, one in South America, one in London, one in France, one in the Middle East and one in the Far East. Their identities were unknown to the President and the source of their funding was concealed. They seem to be very high-level intelligence operatives with considerable freedom of action and extensive funds. Who does control them has never been revealed.

The person connected with Holmes who revealed to him the identity of Pericles Craig must have been Mycroft Holmes. For some reason, Holmes had not, at this point, revealed Mycroft's existence to Watson. He did so later in the same year in the matter of 'The Greek Interpreter'.

CHAPTER NINE

Watson's unlikely acquaintances at the Green Dragon were real. They all worked for the old *Sporting Times* – 'the Pink 'Un'. Major (later Lieutenant-Colonel) Newnham-Davis was perhaps the oddest of the bunch; a commissioned officer who hankered after the stage and took courses in drama and scene-painting while serving his Queen. He left the Army and joined the *Sporting Times*, to return to the colours on the outbreak of World War I. His extraordinary nickname (which also became his by-line in the paper) arose when he volunteered, too late, for a part in a charity pantomime. He was told that he could hide beneath the stage and, if anyone forgot their lines, emerge crying, 'I am the Dwarf of Blood!' A certain John B. Booth joined the paper at seventeen, from a solicitor's office, and lived well into this century, publishing remarkable volumes of reminiscence about the sporting, theatrical, royal, criminal and other personalities of late-Victorian and Edwardian England. I freely acknowledge that I have often found his works a useful check on some of Watson's descriptions.

The horse Merry Hampton was owned by George Alexander Baird who used the name 'Mr Abingdon' on race courses. The horse's name seems to have been an example of Baird's bawdy humour – the Stewards once insisted that he change the name of a two-year-old colt before it could be registered. He had put forward 'Cockrow, by Peter out of Maid of Perth'. As a boy he inherited several fortunes but spent his time hanging around racing stables. He walked out of Eton and Cambridge and eventually took up riding under the tutelage of the great Fred Archer. His conduct on the course caused problems and he was 'warned off' for two years, after which he bought and trained first-class horses, winning the Two Thousand Guineas, the Oaks and the Derby. He was well disliked in racing circles for his misbehaviour and his arrogance – one contemporary called him 'a dyed-in-the-wool swine'. Interested also in prize-fighting, he died at thirty-two in a New Orleans hotel surrounded by bare-fist fighters.

John Wilkes Booth alive in London, twenty-two years after Lincoln's assassination? The official record shows that Booth was shot by a Union soldier at Garrett's Farm, Virginia, days after the death of Lincoln, but even that bastion of cautious rectitude, *Encyclopaedia Britannica*, adds a question mark after the date and place of his death.

There have been persistent stories that, like his co-conspirator John Surratt, Booth escaped to England. Surratt drifted to many countries including Egypt (where he was betrayed) and eventually returned to America; rumours say that Booth lived in England and in India (under the name of John Byron Wilkes, David E. George or John St Helen), returning at last to America where he died in the early years of this century. The man killed at Garrett's Farm is supposed to have been a former Confederate agent working for the War Department called Captain James William Boyd.

Four of Booth's co-conspirators, Lewis Paine, George Atzerodt, David Herold and Mary Surratt, were hanged and others imprisoned including the hapless Dr Mudd who treated Booth's broken ankle after the assassination and was sentenced to the Dry Tortugas. He is the subject of two movies.

Booth's account of the murder of Lincoln is neither impossible nor improbable. As, in our own time, President John F. Kennedy was almost certainly the victim of a conspiracy hatched and led by his Director of the FBI, J. Edgar Hoover, so many historians have pointed the finger at Lincoln's Secretary of War, Edwin Stanton, as the architect of the President's murder.

A public dispute occurred over Booth's diary. Stanton claimed that there were eighteen pages missing when it was handed to his Department, but Lafayette Baker, head of the Secret Service, claimed that it had been intact. Twenty-five years ago the missing pages were found, in the possession of a descendant of Stanton. They detail contacts between Booth and officials of the Union in the period before the assassination.

A bizarre footnote to the affair – when an elderly American claimed on his deathbed that he was Booth, the undertaker recalled that there was an unclaimed reward for Booth and refused to bury him. The embalmed corpse is still in the possession of a private owner in America who, presumably, hopes one day to claim the reward.

For a painstaking study of the anomalies in the Lincoln assassination I recommend Otto Eisenshiml's *Why Was Lincoln Murdered?* (Faber and Faber, 1937). More modern material can be found in *The Lincoln Conspiracy* by David Balsiger and Charles E. Sellier Jr. (Schick Sunn Classic Books, California, 1977).

An irritating feature of Watson's narratives is his practice of using a mixture of real names and fictitious ones, but in this case it is possible, I believe, to identify one disguised character. The name 'Sempford Candover' appears to be a thin concealment for Sandford Conover, who played the part in the attempt to hang Jefferson Davis described by Essex and may have played the part in the Lincoln plot described by Booth. Eisenschiml (see above) describes him as 'an amusing scoundrel' who 'lied fluently and plausibly'. Nat Brandt, in *The Man Who Tried to Burn New York* (Berkley Books, New York, 1990) calls Conover 'totally untrustworthy'.

The phrase, 'A Confederate doing duty upon his own responsibility' comes from a letter left by Booth in an attempt to establish that he acted alone in killing Lincoln.

If it is possible to establish that the present manuscript is really the work of John H. Watson, the reference to Booth's wife and family may be the key. Booth is usually presented as unmarried, but he was, in fact, secretly married to an actress called Izola Darcy (stage name Martha Mills). They have living descendants. It is in the highest degree unlikely that Watson could have known this unless Booth told him so.

CHAPTER TWENTY

Buffalo Bill – Colonel William F. Cody – turned his amazingly adventurous life into entertainment, first by appearing as himself in melodramatic plays, and later when he launched his Wild West Show.

The show came to the American Exhibition at Kensington in 1887 and almost upstaged Victoria's Golden Jubilee. It was an instant success with the British public and was visited by everybody of any consequence, including the Queen herself. She was so delighted with it that she ordered a special performance for her royal guests at Windsor on 20 June 1887, the eve of her Jubilee celebration.

That Cody's London rooms were adjacent to those of the *New York Herald*'s Blumenthal was probably no accident. Blumenthal worshipped Cody (he said that Buffalo Bill and Robin Hood were his two great childhood heroes) and sent reams of copy back to the States, describing Cody's overwhelming success in Britain.

Nate Salisbury was Cody's partner in the show and Major Burke his manager.

CHAPTER TWENTY-TWO

A major feature of Cody's show were dramatic representations of an Indian attack upon a wagon train, an Indian attack on settlers' cabins and an Indian attack upon the Deadwood stage-coach. After the Spanish-American War, Cody added a two-act reconstruction of the storming of San Juan Hill including some of Teddy Roosevelt's Roughriders who had carried out the attack.

The original Deadwood coach and its driver, Johnny Burke, took part in the show, and it was quite usual for prominent members of the audience to play the rescued passengers. The English financier Morton Frewen (nicknamed 'Mortal Ruin') once owned the biggest cattle spread in Wyoming and regularly used the Deadwood stage. When he took his nephews (one of whom was the young Winston Churchill) to see the show in London some of his former cowhands recognised him in the audience and he and the boys were invited to ride the Deadwood stage.

It is definitely the case that Prince Edward and the four kings rode in the coach at Windsor and very probable that Cody made his joke about the royal flush. It seems that Cody recognised a royal flush as four kings and an ace, not the ace to ten of any suit. Another version says that Prince Edward made the joke and that Cody replied that he also held the royal joker.

CHAPTER TWENTY-THREE

Codd's was a brand of lemonade, much approved of by small boys, not so much for its taste as because it came in a glass bottle sealed with a glass ball held in place in the bottle's neck by the gas pressure in the bottle. Smashing the empty bottle released the ball and supplied an excellent glass marble, a treasure when the common marble was made of hardened clay and soon developed irregularities. It was a sarcastic reference to Codd's lemonade compared to beer that gave the English language the word 'codswallop' as an expression of contempt.

Why, precisely, the town of Basingstoke provokes sarcasm and mirth I do not know. W. S. Gilbert wrote it into *Ruddigore* in the expectation of a laugh and, more recently, one recalls a *Private Eye* cartoon with the caption, 'It says here that the people of Basingstoke have no word for Hell'. Evidently the Pink 'Un's men agreed with Gilbert and *Private Eye*. On reflection, if the Dwarf of Blood and the Pitcher were alive today they would probably be writing for *Private Eye*.

Gilbert the carriage driver appears to have been one Richard Gilbert, a London cabbie, who later boasted that he had driven Arthur Binstead about for more than twenty years.

CHAPTERS TWENTY-FOUR AND TWENTY-FIVE

Holmes' ability to keep his enquiries secret was remarkable. While Watson always admitted that there were tales that Holmes would not let him tell, it is remarkable that three astute journalists took part in the attempt to capture Tumbletye and still the story didn't leak out.

John B. Booth, whom I mentioned in the note to Chapter Nine, had not joined the Pink 'Un in 1887, or the tale of Tumbletye's plot would certainly have found its way into one of his many volumes of reminiscence. Apart from anything else, Booth worshipped Holmes. His last book (I believe) was *Palmy Days* (Richards Press, 1957) and its first chapter is called 'The London of Sherlock Holmes'. In it he tells of a foggy day in his boyhood, when he passed through Baker Street with the family coachman:

> As they gazed, someone in a first floor room lit the
> gas, and all of a sudden – thrill of thrills – the
> tall lean figure of a man was momentarily silhouetted
> against the warm glow. Then the blind fell. Boy and man
> still gazed, rapt, for a full minute; then the brougham
> passed on, its occupants firm in the belief that they had
> seen Sherlock Holmes, his very self, pacing his study,
> deep in thought, preparing to foil the infamous
> Moriarty.

and later:

> It was an eerie experience to stand once again after a
> lapse of some sixty years, in utterly familiar surroundings.
>   'Yes,' I murmured, as I glanced slowly round Sherlock
> Holmes' room in Baker Street, reconstructed for the
> Festival of Britain, 'how well I remember it! It seems
> only yesterday that...'

Booth never tells us about that yesterday, but has he already confirmed that he had been in 221b and known that famous sitting-room? Who knows? He was certainly a friend of Watson's friend Conan Doyle. Did neither Pitcher nor the Dwarf ever tell him about their own adventures with Holmes? If they did he took the story to the grave with him.

CHAPTER TWENTY-SIX

Holmes' observations on Queen Victoria are nothing but the truth. In her prime, Victoria had been the subject of scurrilous ballads about the size of her family ('Do it no more, Do it no more, Oh, the Queen and Prince Albert should do it no more'). After being attacked by press and public for all the reasons he states (and others) she suddenly became enormously popular with the mob at the time of her Jubilees.

185

Watson has done posterity an enormous favour by preserving the details of the Fenian plot against the Jubilee in 1887, for it is known from the memoirs of police officers but no details have survived (other than the fact that Scotland Yard foiled it!). However, he hardly does justice to Tumbletye's later appearance in London.

In 1956 Douglas G. Browne published *The Rise of Scotland Yard* (Harrap, 1956), in which he claimed that he was shown information by the Metropolitan Police indicating that Sir Melville Macnaghten, Commissioner in the 1890s, had identified Jack the Ripper with the originator of a Fenian plot 'to assassinate Mr Balfour at the Irish Office'. Although no confirmation of Browne's statement has ever come to light, if such a memo or report existed it could only refer to Dr Tumbletye for reasons set out below.

Early in the series of East End murders, a coroner fed the press a story about an American doctor who was at large in London and had been attempting to buy women's organs from the dissecting schools of hospitals. It is in the highest degree unlikely that two mad American doctors with the same unsavoury collecting habits were in London that autumn and this too must be a reference to Tumbletye.

Searchers for Jack the Ripper have long striven to identify both Browne's Fenian assassin and the coroner's mad doctor. Stewart Evans and Paul Gainey succeeded in doing so in a book called *The Lodger: The Arrest and Escape of Jack the Ripper* (Century, 1995). In 1993 a dealer offered Stewart Evans some letters which included one from Chief Inspector Littlechild to his friend George R. Sims, journalist, poet and author of *In the Workhouse, Christmas Day*. Written in 1913 the letter refers to a 'Dr T' and goes on:

> He was an American quack named Tumbletye and was at one time a frequent visitor to London and on these occasions frequently brought under the notice of the police, there being a large dossier concerning him at Scotland Yard. Although a 'Sycopathia [sic] sexualis' subject he was not known as a 'sadist' (which the murderer unquestionably was) but his feelings towards women were remarkable and

bitter in the extreme, a fact on record. Tumbletye was arrested at the time of the murders in connection with unnatural offences and charged at Marlborough Street, remanded on bail, jumped his bail, and got away to Boulogne. He shortly left Boulogne and was never heard of afterwards. It was believed he committed suicide but certain it is that from this time the 'Ripper' murders came to an end.

Stewart Evans and Paul Gainey, starting from this astonishing letter, have revealed much of the bizarre career of Tumbletye in their book, including the fact that he did not commit suicide. Tumbletye died in St Louis in May 1903, a wealthy man.

From the above extract of the Littlechild letter it is evident that Littlechild did not think Tumbletye was the Ripper and there are other good reasons for rejecting him. Watson clearly did not think so, believing that the whole affair was a ruse of Littlechild's to drive the mad doctor out of Britain.

Is it not evident that Tumbletye, having escaped in 1887, returned to Britain the following year, probably with some new plot (perhaps, indeed, to murder Mr Balfour)? While he would have been of interest again to Littlechild and the Secret Department, he was of no consequence to Chief Inspector Swanson's Division at the Yard who were trying to catch the Ripper – of no consequence, that is, until the coroner launched his tale of a mad American doctor. Then Littlechild (who could not deport the Canadian-born madman as 'undesirable') suddenly found a perfect way to drive Tumbletye out of Britain for ever and cover up the signal failures of his Department in the Jubilee plot.

I recommend Evans and Gainey's book to you for further details of Tumbletye. Littlechild resigned from Scotland Yard in 1893 and became a private detective (strange in the light of his offensive remarks to Holmes!). In that capacity he was used by the prosecution to drum up additional evidence against Oscar Wilde.

There may well be other details of this narrative that would bear close examination, but Watson's knowledge of John Wilkes Booth (and, in particular, Booth's secret marriage) go a long way to convince me that we have here an authentic manuscript of Watson's.

Barrie Roberts
June 1998